A DIG IN TIME

ALSO BY PENI R. GRIFFIN

Otto From Otherwhere

A DIG IN TIME

Peni R. Griffin

MARGARET K. McELDERRY BOOKS
NEW YORK

Collier Macmillan Canada
TORONTO

Maxwell Macmillan International Publishing Group
NEW YORK   OXFORD   SINGAPORE   SYDNEY

To my own Gramma,
who never uses tobacco or embarrasses me

Copyright © 1991 by Peni R. Griffin

Margaret K. McElderry Books
Macmillan Publishing Company
866 Third Avenue
New York, NY 10022

Collier Macmillan Canada, Inc.
1200 Eglinton Avenue East
Suite 200
Don Mills, Ontario M3C 3N1

First edition
Printed in the United States of America
10   9   8   7   6   5   4   3   2   1
Library of Congress Cataloging-in-Publication Data
Griffin, Peni R.
A dig in time / by Peni R. Griffin. — 1st ed.
p.   cm.
Summary: While spending the summer with their grandmother in San
Antonio, Texas, twelve-year-old Nan and her younger brother find
artifacts buried in the yard and discover how to use them to travel
back through time to significant moments in their family history.
ISBN 0–689–50525–6
[1. Time travel—Fiction.   2. Grandmothers—Fiction.   3. Family
life—Fiction.   4. San Antonio (Tex.)—Fiction.]   I. Title.
PZ7.G88136Di   1991
[Fic]—dc20   90–47388

Contents

1

The Spirit of the Place

Nan knew where she was before she opened her eyes. She had kicked the covers off, but the morning air lay warm and heavy on top of her, as it only could in Texas. During the three weeks between her parents' departure for the Middle East and the end of school, she had wakened each morning in her aunt's air-conditioned modern house, anticipating her visit to Gramma, and now she was here. Music played downstairs, indicating that Gramma must be up already.

The room her mother had grown up in snapped into focus when Nan put on her glasses. Books and photographs nearly hid the white walls, and the honey-colored wood floor was bare. The alarm clock on the nightstand said it was ten after seven. Feeling virtuous, Nan made her bed and padded down the hall to the bathroom. The door of Aunt Hope's old room stood open, and she could see her little brother, Tim, asleep at the foot of the narrow bed. She was tempted to get a glass of water and dump it on him, but that didn't fit her mood. There'd be plenty of time for that later in the summer.

Grampa had been a professional photographer, and the walls were covered with his work. Lots of family pictures, of course, but also what Mom called "art shots," and these led Nan to dawdle on her way down to breakfast. She had one on her wall at home—a cypress reflected in water, taken from some peculiar angle so that the tree and the reflection seemed joined at the root, and the tops of each seemed to continue out of sight. *Infinitree* was the name of that one; and there were many similar works here, playing with angles and perspective. Nan studied pictures with names like *Bluebonnet Jungle, Stairway to Heaven* (it took a minute to recognize, with a start of pleasure, the stairs she was on), and *Rose-Colored Glasses*, skipping over the portraits of aunts, uncles, and cousins of whose existence she was only marginally aware.

The picture at the bottom of the stairway, just where the light from the open back door hit it, was invisible because of the glare until she stood directly in front of it, and it took her a minute to sort out the picture from her own reflection on the glass. The typed label on the frame read *The Spirit of the Place*, but it was just a black-and-white picture of the front of the house. Her reflection matched up with it in an interesting way—her nose running along the door, her mouth matching the line of the

2

step, and her eyes even with the porch lamps—but you couldn't credit Grampa with that. Nan turned away and noticed from the corner of her eye that her reflection did not move with her.

Spooked, she looked again. Sure enough, a ghostly face stared out at her—her own face—no, that was silly. Nan pushed her glasses firmly up her nose. She'd grown used to herself without glasses in the months since she'd gotten contact lenses, but she was wearing glasses now, and the face in the picture wasn't. She had had to wear glasses for as long as she could remember and hadn't even gotten the contacts till after Grampa died. That was just somebody with a square face composed mostly of straight lines, as hers was, superimposed on the house by means of a double exposure.

Now she could actually see what had been there before she knew how to look. A young man with slicked-back hair faced down the camera, as if the instrument had offered him a challenge. Nan rather liked his lack of a smile. She had frowned into many camera lenses herself. Probably this man had had better things to do than stand still and let Grampa make his picture. She wondered idly who he was.

In the kitchen, a radio played and bacon hissed. "Good morning, sugardoodle!" Gramma stopped singing along with the radio to swoop across the kitchen and give Nan a tight, pillowy hug, smelling of stale tobacco and fresh biscuits. Nan hugged back. She was almost as tall as Gramma now and could reach around her neck. "You're just in time," said Gramma, whirling to lift the bacon onto a platter. "Need you to set the table and butter those biscuits. Tim in the bathroom?"

"In bed," said Nan, getting the plates down from the glass-doored cupboard. "He sleeps late, you know."

"Not in my house he doesn't," declared Gramma, turning off the blue fire under the grits. "I didn't work over a hot stove all morning so he could wander down at all hours and eat everything stone cold." She paused to survey the array of dishes she had out, a slight frown twisting the corners of her mouth. "I might shouldn't've made quite so much breakfast, now I come to look at it. It was so much fun cooking for other people again—and I shudder to think what kind of wimpy Yankee breakfasts that Marian's been feeding you!"

"She likes yogurt and granola," said Nan, busily buttering biscuits. Gramma always called Dad's sister "that Marian," just as Aunt Marian always referred to Gramma as "your grandmother," in a voice like a twist of lemon. Nan didn't know why—something to do with Mom and Dad's wedding, she thought.

Gramma made a face and returned to the eggs. "Hmph! It's a good thing y'all came to me. I bet she's got one of these modern kitchens with a dishwasher and a microwave and no cupboards to speak of."

Nan nodded. "And ferns all over the place. It's awful. You've got the nicest kitchen I know."

4

She did, too. It was bigger than Nan's bedroom at home. The windows were wide open, and they didn't need electric light in the daytime. The kitchenette at home had no windows at all, and nothing in it was farther than three steps from anything else. Nan also liked it that Gramma never redecorated or threw anything away that could be made to serve some function; so she had an old, round-edged refrigerator, and Nan could eat off the same black porcelain table and get cookies from the same Aunt Jemima cookie jar as her mother always had. The newest thing here was the coffee maker Mom and Dad had gotten Gramma for Christmas three years ago. The second newest thing was probably Nan herself.

"Maybe I'll teach you to cook this summer," offered Gramma, carrying the eggs and grits to the table. "Run upstairs and fetch Tim, now. He's had as much sleep as any boy needs."

Nan took the stairs two at a time and hurled herself on top of her brother, aiming for the ticklish spot. "Breakfast's ready!"

Tim rolled off the bed with a squeal of protest. "I'm not asleep! Get off!"

"If you weren't asleep, you should've gotten up," said Nan, standing over him.

Tim had hunched around his stomach to protect the ticklish place. "I was making a poem. Now it's gone and it's your fault."

"You'll make another one," said Nan callously, pulling clothes out of his dresser and throwing them at him. "C'mon, I'm hungry."

"I'm coming. Leave me alone."

Nan stood outside the door urging him to feats of speed and herded him downstairs past the pictures as if he were a recalcitrant calf. Nonetheless, he pulled up in front of *The Spirit of the Place*. "Ooh, look! Grampa took a picture of a ghost!"

"Oh, he did not. That's a double exposure."

"But it says right here. Spirit. A spirit's a ghost."

"There aren't any ghosts, dummy."

"Aunt Marian says there are."

"Daddy says there aren't. You think he'd say that if Grampa'd taken a picture of one?"

That shut him up long enough to get him into the kitchen. Gramma said grace, and then Nan was at last able to set about the serious business of breakfast. She would have to eat more than her share of grits, because Tim didn't like them, and it wouldn't be nice to leave the bowl half full. Nan felt the need for something solid after three weeks of Aunt Marian's cooking, and grits were really pretty tasty once buttered, salted, and mixed up with the scrambled eggs and bacon. Tim got a puny helping of eggs, a big glass of orange juice, and a biscuit, on which he dribbled honey absently. "Gramma," he said, "who's the ghost in the picture on the stairs?"

6

Gramma did not pause in her application of pear preserves to biscuits. "What ghost, honey?"

Nan swallowed a half-chewed mouthful. "He means the *Spirit of the Place* picture. I told him it was just a double exposure."

"It looks like a ghost," said Tim mildly.

"Even if there were ghosts, they wouldn't have heads as big as houses. It's just some cousin, right?"

"No," said Gramma. "It *is* a double exposure, but that's Big Daddy."

Nan stopped eating in surprise. "But—that's a young picture. It doesn't have any wrinkles or anything."

"This is true. Grampa didn't take that part of the picture." Gramma smiled, and for a minute her sharp, dark eyes looked as vague as Tim's hazel ones. "After Big Daddy died we were going through his things, and we found some old camera equipment. Papa Mort—that was Big Daddy's daddy—used to get fads all the time, and 'long about the time they built this house, he got a fad for photography. It didn't last—none of his hobbies ever did—and here we found this old, old Brownie, with some negatives that hadn't ever been printed! I never saw Persh—I never saw your grampa so excited except when our babies were born. I don't know how long it took him to get that *Spirit of the Place* picture to come out right. When he saw how he could make the face match up to the front of the house— my! He was pleased with himself when it came out right!"

7

"My face matches up to the house, too," said Nan. "I thought it was my reflection at first."

"Doesn't surprise me a lick. You're the spitting image of Big Daddy. Said that the first time ever I saw you."

Tim had been nibbling his biscuit and staring thoughtfully into space all this time. "If our great-grampa was Big Daddy," he said now, not focusing his eyes, "did that make Grampa Little Daddy?"

Nan thought this was a silly question, but Gramma took it seriously enough. "Grampa didn't think so. Your great-uncle Stanley, now, the man that married my big sister, Becky, he felt that way for sure. Big Daddy was going to let him into the building business, but Stan dragged poor Becky off to New Mexico, just as soon as he got back from the war, away from her kin and all, just because he didn't want to call his father-in-law 'sir' at work." A hard note had crept into her voice; she softened it as abruptly as Mom shifting gears in the pickup. "Your Grampa liked Big Daddy. He said most people weren't any good for pictures because they just had faces. You could look at them all day and never know who they were. He said when you looked at Big Daddy, you knew you were looking at the boss man."

The boss man. Nan buried a stubborn piece of butter in her grits so it would melt faster. It had always embarrassed her slightly to have someone in the family called Big Daddy—it sounded so hick, like something from those TV shows Mom complained about in which the whole

8

South was shown as a land of corny drawls and corrupt sheriffs. The way Gramma said it, though, the name had a certain dignity. "Did everybody call him Big Daddy?" she asked.

"Land, yes! Even the workmen—when he was around it was 'Mr. Chadwell' this and 'the boss' that, but I remember once when I had to take some plans over to a site because he couldn't go, the foreman took them and asked me, 'What's the matter with Big Daddy?' Just like one of his own kin." Tim scooted his chair back, and she was on him immediately. "Where you think you're going?"

Tim pointed at his empty juice glass, half-eaten biscuit, and scraps of egg. "I'm finished."

"I didn't hear you excuse yourself. Besides, you can eat more than that. You just finish up that biscuit, now."

They were going to go through this a lot this summer, Nan could tell. She reached for another biscuit, thinking about the previous owner of her face. Big Daddy. She felt a little tickle of pride behind her breastbone. Everybody'd called him Big Daddy, and she was just like him.

2
Grampa's Pipe

*B*ig Daddy had built his house on what passed, in San Antonio, for a creek. To Nan it looked like a ditch, though there was a syrupy streak of water down the middle. The ditch part was maybe ten times as wide as the water part, and even the water was almost lost among tall grass. There wasn't so much as a bridge over it along this stretch— streets just dead-ended into it and resumed on the other side. Tim and Nan stood on the bank under the bright, empty sky. A group of brown children with black hair played tag farther down the creek bed.

"This is a pretty crummy creek," said Tim. "It ought to have water up to the edge and trees and frogs and things."

"There's probably frogs if you go right down there," said Nan. "Maybe it'll rain. Gramma says it gets full when it rains."

10

Tim looked back at the house. The sewing machine chattered from its downstairs room. "It's too hot to play," he said. "You think she'd mind if I read instead? I found a book in my room last night."

"I guess she won't care as long as you're getting fresh air and sunshine," said Nan, after a moment's consideration. She could have made him play with her, but she wasn't sure what she wanted to play, and she'd just had a neat idea. A pecan tree grew right past her bedroom window—the window that didn't have a screen. All she needed was a boost and an excuse. "She didn't want us running in and out while she was working, though. Why don't you climb that tree and get your book that way?"

Tim's face paled satisfactorily. "I can't climb trees."

"Sure you can! I'll just give you a boost to the first branch, and the rest is easy. You can get in the window to my room."

Tim swallowed. "Why don't you do it?"

"It's your book."

"But you're good at climbing trees. Please?"

"Oh—all right," said Nan, as if that hadn't been what she intended all along. "You'll have to give me a boost, though."

"I hate giving boosts. You're too heavy." Tim trailed after her to the tree.

"Then you'll just have to do it yourself."

He sighed and bent down. "Okay. If you break my back you have to pay to fix it."

After three or four tries she made it to the high cleft where the branches started, and then it was easy till she came level with the window. A squirrel sat on the roof, making indignant noises at her. "Oh, shut up," she told it, gripping the branch she was on with her knees and studying the route. From here the distance seemed greater and more perilous than it had from below, and the ground was uncomfortably distant. The second story of the house was smaller than the first story, so there was a rim of roof to step on if she needed it.

"Maybe it's too far," called Tim helpfully.

"I can do it," snapped Nan. "What's this book look like?"

"It's on the nightstand. You'll find it."

The pause had been long enough for her to gather her nerve. She leaned across the void, gripped the windowsill with both hands, brought one knee over, had a bad minute of balancing in space, and half crawled, half somersaulted clumsily into her room. The thump with which she landed was louder than she'd intended and hurt her knees.

The book on Tim's nightstand was perilously old and coming loose from its bindings. Nan looked at the inside cover. Papa Mort had given it to Gramma for her eighth birthday. Gramma would kill them if this got damaged. She made sure her T-shirt was tucked securely into her shorts, put the book down her front, and climbed back out the window. It was even scarier from this side, but now she knew she could do it; and besides, she couldn't fail in front of Tim.

"You be careful with this," Nan said sternly when she reached the ground, untucking her shirt and pulling the book out. "You didn't tell me it was nearly as old as Gramma."

"I'm always careful," said Tim, fitting himself into the shady roots of the pecan and opening the book.

Nan wandered around the yard, sweating. What should she do now? She found Gramma's big cat, Satchmo (named after Gramma's favorite musician), on the back steps; but he was not playful and soon got tired of being petted. She considered approaching the children in the creek, but found she didn't much want to. She wasn't shy—of course not—but it was hot for tag, and she didn't want to butt in. She examined the fig tree by the shed, but the wasps had already started on the only fruit on it that looked ripe enough to eat. She pulled that one off, getting a squirt of milky juice on her knuckles, and threw it toward the creek, misjudging the force of the toss so that it bounced and disappeared among the ragged plants where Grampa had kept his garden.

Nan went into the garden shed. A bright lizard scurried out of the middle of the floor to freeze behind a dusty bottle of plant food. She had forgotten the woody, earthy, cool smell of the shed till she walked into it. Suddenly she was sad about Grampa. She had stayed with Grampa

13

and Gramma only once before that she could recall, when she had been six, and Grampa had let her tag after him while he took care of the garden. She remembered the dry, soft dirt under her fingers. She remembered the stool tucked into the corner of the shed. He had sat on it mixing fertilizer one day, making a hideous stench and talking about growing things. "Anything'll grow if you let it," he said.

Nan was too sad to stay here, but she also had an idea. She gathered up the hoe, the trowel, and the small tool like a claw, and carried them over to Grampa's garden. The border of gray timber that marked it off from the rest of the yard had shifted, settling deeper into the ground and pulling itself out of line. What wasn't bare ground was mostly weeds and last year's dead stalks, but some tomatoes had come up on their own (mavericks, Gramma called them) escaping into the yard and down the creek bank. Nan frowned at the mess. Probably the first thing to do was to pull up the dead stuff.

The work was harder than she remembered, and soon her knees and back itched with sweat. Some of the plants were too tough for her—the cornstalks, for instance, would bend but not break, and tore up her hands. This made her victories over the dry remains of beans and peas more satisfying. She would have to get the scythe out and cut down the cornstalks, she planned, if Gramma would let her use it. She whistled "The Yellow Rose of Texas," as Grampa had taught her, and then tried the march from

Bridge on the River Kwai, but couldn't get it right. She rubbed an itch on her forehead with the back of her hand.

Nan found that the plants came up more easily when she loosened the soil around their roots with the claw first. She was hacking away at the cucumbers and thinking about getting a drink from the outdoor faucet when she hit something hard. Assuming it was a rock (though the rocks around here were mostly white and this was dark brown), she dug the claw in and turned it over.

It was Grampa's pipe—the banged-up one that he took along fishing or working outdoors. The sight of the amber mouthpiece and smooth bowl all crusted with dirt gave her a rush of sadness even worse than the smell in the shed had; but this was followed at once by a thrill. She had dug up a relic of the past—just as Mom and Dad were doing in the Mideast right now. It was a small, intimate relic, not as impressive as bowls and tablets from before Jesus was born; but it couldn't be any less special. Carefully she broke the dirt off with her fingers and then wiped it with her shirttail. She couldn't tell if the packed mass in the bowl was dirt or tobacco, so she left it.

Nan sat on her haunches and wiped her wet hair back. The sewing machine still chattered like a locust. She had to show someone, and there was only Tim. Carrying the pipe across the yard as if it were made of glass, she stood over her brother. "Guess what I found."

Tim did not lift his nose from the book. "Ask me if I care."

"You care, all right." She kicked his ankle, not enough to hurt, just enough to make him look up resentfully.

"I'll tell!"

"I found Grampa's pipe buried in the garden," said Nan, thrusting the artifact into his face.

Tim blinked at it. "Why would Grampa bury his pipe?"

"He wouldn't." Nan figured out what had happened as she explained to him. "It must've fallen out of his pocket. Remember at the funeral, Gramma kept talking about how he died? When she came back from the store late he wanted to tell her something that'd happened to him, and she told him to tell her over supper and asked him to pick some cucumbers."

"And she wondered what took him so long and looked out the window, and he was all huddled up on the ground." Tim hunched slightly, as if against a sudden chill. "But how did his pipe get buried?"

"Everything gets buried. That's why Mom and Dad have to dig for old cities. The wind blows dirt over everything and hides it. That's why we have to dust and vacuum every week." That point had never occurred to her before, but it explained why Mom was so picky about those things being done regularly.

"The ground must've been a lot thinner, a long time ago." Tim lifted the pipe from her hands. Normally she would have closed her fist on it—she'd found it, after all—but his face had folded in on itself, and a small crease appeared between his eyebrows. Most of the time, his face

16

was as vague and blank as a doll's. When that crease appeared, it meant that he was making poetry, and, if left alone, would have something to show for his efforts in a half hour or so. Nan could always get the pipe back then. She was the only person she knew with a poet in the family. The hairs rose on his arms as he stroked the bowl of the pipe.

"This is creepy," he said. "Grampa's pipe is here, but Grampa's gone."

"I don't see anything creepy about it. His pictures are here, too."

"But they weren't buried. This was buried just like Grampa was." He studied it on all sides, as if something about it puzzled him. Nan returned to the garden.

She began turning over the cucumber bed more carefully, alert for anything else that might have fallen with the pipe. She found some snail shells, a few dirt-stiff pieces of paper and plastic that must have blown there on the wind, and a couple of the seed packets fastened to stakes with which Grampa had marked the garden beds. Dust got under a contact, and she had a brief period of agony trying to blink it out. She was sitting on her heels, one grubby finger pressed to her eyelid (but not rubbing it; she knew better than to rub her eyes with her contacts in) and tears tickling down her cheeks, when Tim came over.

"I made a poem," he announced shyly, "but I couldn't write it down without going inside."

"Say it, then," said Nan, releasing the pressure on her eyeball and blinking experimentally. Good, she'd done it.

Tim cleared his throat, clasped his hands in front of him, and turned his toes out. Some book or other about a one-room schoolhouse had convinced him that this was the proper position in which to recite poetry.

"Grampa's pipe is here, but Grampa's gone.
Nan didn't find him, digging up the weeds
he can't dig up now. It was not so long
ago he came here every day to plant his seeds.

Grampa's dead, and I can't cry enough.
Grampa was buried, and his pipe was, too.
Time will bury every kind of stuff.
His seeds were buried. Difference was, they grew."

Nan was impressed. "That's good," she said. "I like it when you make poetry that's all true. A lot of the time you stick in too much pretend stuff."

"Long and gone don't rhyme, really," said Tim, seriously. "You think that's all right?"

"It's just fine!" Nan declared. "I hope you remember it long enough to put it in your notebook."

"You want to learn it, too? Then you could help me remember what to write down."

Nan's English teacher had told her she had a good memory, so she was not going to turn down a chance to dem-

18

onstrate. She made him repeat the poem line by line twice, saying each one after him; then she closed her eyes and said the whole thing over with him, thinking about what the words said. Words were easier to remember when you knew exactly what they meant. "Nan didn't find him, digging in the weeds—" That was true. Of course, she hadn't been looking for him—not exactly—but, now she thought about it, maybe she had been, in a sideways way. "His seeds were buried. Difference was, they grew." She had not begun to think about the feeling it made in her, when a peculiar rippling sensation ran from her head to her heels. Her eyes blinked open.

The sun was heavy and hot on her head. Locusts were loud all round, but the tall, green cornstalks, the rangy tomatoes, the low, compact rows of beans and peas and carrots, made no sound or movement in the still air. Grampa stood between the rows of runner beans, his back to them, hoeing rhythmically. His white hair poked out from under his baseball cap—no, his gimme cap; he'd always called it a gimme cap—and she could see the pale brown spots on the back of his neck. He was whistling "The Yellow Rose of Texas" in the clear, low whistle she knew so well.

3

Without Rules

*N*an jumped as something clutched her hand. It was only Tim, his eyes round as soup spoons. Locusts chattered all around, but she couldn't hear the sewing machine or the voices of the children in the creek. Grampa reached the end of the row, not three feet away, leaned on his hoe, and took his bandanna out of his hip pocket. He saw them as he wiped his forehead, then started, the wrinkles spreading around his face like rays round a sun. "Kids! What are y'all doing here?" He dropped the hoe to sweep both of them into a hug—solid, warm, and slippery with sweat.

Nan was too surprised to do anything but hug him back, but Tim squawked and tugged backward on her hand. A train hooted somewhere. Another ripple worked its way from her heels to her head, and Grampa whirled out of her hands as the world broke apart like the view through a kaleidoscope. Dizzy and sick, Nan sat down suddenly. A bird called—*cu-ru-cu!*—and the chatter of the sewing machine resumed, but the train whistle and the locusts ceased abruptly. Dry cornstalks rustled against each other in the breeze. Tim's hand was clammy, and he shivered.

Nan felt like crying, so she turned on him. "What did you do? You spoiled it!"

Tim stopped shivering, and said in grim triumph, "I told you there were ghosts."

"You are so stupid! There aren't any ghosts."

"Yes, there are!" Tim pounded the ground emphatically. "You saw Grampa's ghost, same as me!"

"Oh, and ghost cornstalks, and ghost locusts, and ghost train whistles, too, huh?" Again, the act of explaining to Tim made it all clear to her. "If anybody was ghosts, it was us. We went back in time, dummy! It wasn't Grampa come back from the dead, it was us going back to when he was alive."

"But people don't go back in time. If they did Mom and Dad wouldn't have to dig places up."

"Something special must've happened this once." Nan scowled at the tomato plants, reconstructing the event. "Maybe your poem was some kind of accidental spell."

"I thought you didn't believe in magic."

"I believe in evidence," said Nan loftily, borrowing an argument she had heard Mom use when she changed her mind. "The evidence suggests we traveled back in time —hey! I bet we were what Grampa wanted to talk to Gramma about!"

"Huh?"

"He saw us, too, didn't he? But he knew we weren't in Texas, and then when we blinked out—He must've been afraid we were ghosts or something. And this must've happened the day he died, or he would've had time to tell Gramma about it, and we'd already know he saw us. She *said* he had something to tell her that day."

"Oh." Tim's voice sounded smaller than usual. "You think maybe we scared him to death?"

Nan tossed this nasty thought away promptly. "Don't be dumb. When we saw him it was the middle of the afternoon and he was hoeing. When he died it was right before supper and he was picking cucumbers. I bet we could've spent the whole afternoon with him if you hadn't pulled me away."

"Bet we couldn't."

"We'll never know now, will we?"

"We could if we did it again."

Nan was both surprised and annoyed that Tim had thought of this before she had. "You'd just spoil it again."

"No I wouldn't! Not now I know what's going on. You're sure he wasn't a ghost?"

"Of course I'm sure." Nan stood up, brushing off the seat of her shorts. "It can't hurt to try."

They both said the poem again, Nan sitting once more and Tim standing, as they had been. Nan squeezed her eyes so tight she felt her contacts against the undersides of her lids; but after two or three tries she felt no ripple and heard no locusts. The sound of the sewing machine ceased. Shortly afterward the back door banged.

"Y'all got some mail," announced Gramma. "Good night, Nan! What happened to you? You look like you been rolling in a hog waller!"

"I started digging up Grampa's garden."

"Good for you. I should've done that last fall, but I didn't have the heart. Too late to grow anything in it now, but at least it doesn't have to look so trashy."

"She found Grampa's pipe," said Tim, holding it out to her. "And I made a spell about it."

"Well, land's sake," said Gramma gently, taking the pipe. "You know, I never thought to go looking for this. He must've had it in his shirt pocket when—what do you mean, a spell? You mean a poem?"

"It started out being a poem but it turned into a spell," Tim explained. "We were just now trying to use it to go back in time and see Grampa again."

Gramma blinked twice and frowned. "I don't think that's a very good game to play, sugar. Once time goes by you can't get it back, and you shouldn't play with spells, anyway."

"But we weren't—" Nan began.

"I know you didn't mean anything by it," interrupted Gramma. "But lots of things start out as games and turn serious. It's better just not to have anything to do with magic, even for pretend. Come on in now, and you can read that letter to Tim and me. It's from Mom and Dad."

Nan had been about to explain some more, but now she hurried inside, Tim on her heels, and found the blue airmail envelope on top of a pile of bills and sale flyers on the kitchen table. She tried to tear off one end neatly, like Mom did, but it wouldn't tear straight and she nearly mutilated the letter. Tim hung over her shoulder. Gramma started making chili.

Mom's letters were always interesting. She wrote about the things they were finding, and the camp animals, and the people on the dig—both the ones who had come thousands of miles to dig up broken dishes, and the ones who had lived there all their lives without suspecting the wealth of history under their feet. Dad had drawn funny pictures in the margins, showing how Mom looked in a native headdress, and how he had bravely fought off a terrorist raid by goats. "Hmm!" snorted Gramma, covering the chili pot and pulling a cigarette out of her skirt pocket. "They shouldn't joke about terrorists. That's a dangerous part of the world."

"I bet digging in the Mideast isn't any more dangerous than smoking in Texas," said Nan.

"You watch that smart mouth of yours, young lady," said Gramma, lighting the cigarette in the low blue flame on the stove.

"I'm not smarting off," said Nan. "People shouldn't smoke."

"When you're as much older than me as I am than you, then you can tell me what I shouldn't do." The smoke

24

tainted the savory chili smell. "When you write Mom and Dad, you going to tell them you're digging up artifacts, too?"

"Uh-huh," said Nan, struck by an idea. "Can I have a dig in the backyard? If we can't get a good garden anymore anyway?"

Gramma blew smoke out. "Hmm. I don't know why not. Just there around the garden, though—I don't want you tearing up the whole yard. I wonder if Indians ever stayed on this creek? It'd be keen to dig up some real arrowheads."

"Arrowheads!" Tim's face lit up.

"Don't get your hopes up, now! Mostly it's just going to be modern stuff, since the house was built, if you find anything. You might not, you know."

"Modern stuff's okay," Tim assured her. "You want to hear what I wrote about the pipe?"

Nan realized that Tim had left his book outside and slipped off to retrieve it as he was reciting. Then she surveyed her proposed digging site. Clearing the dead plants would be a lot of work. She'd about worn herself out, and the amount she had accomplished seemed pitifully small. It'd be worth any amount of work, though, if they could slip backward in time again!

She had gotten thoroughly dirty that morning, and Gramma made her wash her face and legs as well as her hands before lunch. As she sat with her legs in the tub, Tim passed his hands under the faucet in the sink and asked, in a small voice, "Was it bad of me to make a spell?"

"Of course not." Nan scrubbed her knee. "Even if spells are bad, you didn't know you were making one. Anyway, it can't be honest-to-God magic."

"But you said—"

"Oh, I didn't have any better word, that's all," said Nan airily. She had thought this out completely by now. "It's got to all be scientific, really. Everything is. Magic is just science before you figure out the rules." She turned on the cold water and rinsed her legs while soaping her arms.

"Then why won't Gramma believe me? I tried to tell her what happened, but she thought it was a game."

"If it'd happened just to you and I hadn't seen it myself, I wouldn't believe you, either," Nan admitted. "We'll have to learn the rules, that's all. I'll dig things up, and you can make poems about them, and we'll see if we can time travel again. Then once we know how to do it any time we want to, we'll show Gramma, and she'll have to believe us."

"Hey! That's a good idea! And then we can show Mom and Dad—"

"Listen! We can teach them to do it, too! They won't have to do so much guessing!" A glorious vista of possibility opened before her. "They can dig something up that they don't know what it was for, and go back and watch people use it! They can even talk to them—they can talk

26

to people that lived before Bible days and find out everything about them and write books and papers and everything, better than all the professors ever wrote. They'll be
famous!"

"And then everybody'll ask how they do it, and they'll
say, 'Our kids discovered time travel'! We'll be famous,
too!"

"We can teach classes how to do it and charge lots of
money." Nan turned off the water and leaned drippily
across the floor for a towel. "We'll all be rich, and we'll
go live in one of those big fancy houses, like the professors
live in, instead of that poky old apartment. It'll be great!"

"Your chili's getting cold!" called Gramma. "I said
wash, not go swimming!"

Nan dried off hurriedly and ran downstairs after Tim,
her head fizzing with plans.

4
The Story of the Flood

Gramma would not let Nan use the scythe and said she wasn't such a fool as to use it herself, at her age, with her heart, in this heat. Despite Nan's best efforts, the garden remained too overgrown to dig for most of a week, until Cousin Stella and her husband, Bob, came to dinner.

Stella didn't look like a member of the family, with her curly hair, big eyes, and delicate face. Nan had a vague memory of being baby-sat by her, and had seen her crying at Grampa's funeral till her pretty eyes were red, puffy, and streaked with mascara; other than that, she knew nothing about her.

Bob had been with her at the funeral, but they hadn't been married at that time. Nan found herself obscurely embarrassed to look at him. She wasn't a shy person, so the problem couldn't be that. She had nothing but scorn for girls who got all soft-kneed because some boy or other was good looking—much less a grown-up man!—so it couldn't be that. She wasn't prejudiced against Mexicans, or anybody else—certainly not!—so it couldn't be that. She kept her eyes on her plate, shoveling down Gramma's chicken fricassee, and feeling hot in the face when he told her that the fruit salad she had made under Gramma's directions was delicious.

After dinner they took their iced tea and sat on metal lawn chairs while Bob fetched the scythe and began clearing away the garden. "I think that's a really neat idea," said Stella. "What do you reckon you'll find?"

"I don't know," said Nan. "That's what you dig to find out."

"You never know," said Gramma. "Might be anything. When the creek's high, things tend to catch on that point where the garden is from all over."

"Good thing for us," said Stella.

"How come?" asked Tim, looking up from petting Satchmo.

"Because that's where the tree was that saved Gramma's life," said Stella. "Right in back of the root vegetables."

"What tree?"

"My land, didn't your mom ever tell you how I almost drowned?" asked Gramma. "She wanted to hear about it often enough when she was little."

Tim looked at the creek, and looked at Gramma. "You didn't almost drown in that creek. It doesn't have enough water."

29

"Oh, it did that night!" Gramma pulled out her cigarettes and lighter. "It was the biggest, roaringest old flood that ever came through town."

Whack! Whack! Whack! went the scythe among the cornstalks. Bitter smoke crept onto the warm evening air.

"I wasn't but a couple of weeks old," said Gramma, "but my mama told me about it many a time. The water filled the yard up and came in the first floor, and then it came in the second floor and we had to climb out on the roof. Just like a row of drowning pigeons. There was my big brother Jake, he was five, and my big sister Becky—she was three—and Mama holding me—and Big Daddy, and Polly, the colored girl that helped with us kids, and Mama's cat Sam, and Buglebell the dog. The city hadn't built up so much back then, and we were lots closer to the country. Wasn't anybody in screaming distance of us, so we didn't bother to scream."

Nan seized the opportunity.

"You're not supposed to say people are colored, Gramma. They don't like it. And it's rude to say it if they don't like it."

"I can remember when they liked it just fine," answered Gramma. She paused to breathe smoke. "You want to hear this story, or you want to criticize your elders?"

Nan opened her mouth to explain that she wasn't criticizing, just doing what she thought was right, but Bob paused in his scything and said, "Never mind her, Gramma! You were all sitting on the roof."

30

"All you could see was water and rain. There weren't as many trees back then, mostly just the big live oak that'd been on our property when Big Daddy built this house. The river was running like a freight train, and every now and then a shingle would tear off. Polly asked how long we'd float if the roof came off, and Big Daddy just looked at her and roared, 'If any roof I ever built comes off I'll give you a hundred dollars!'

"But the water was creeping up and up. It wouldn't do them any good to have a solid roof under them if they had water over them. So Big Daddy took a mattress and some bed slats, and whatever he could get his hands on, to start making a raft.

"Becky never did like noise. She started crying, so Polly held her in her lap, and sang 'Papa Gonna Buy You a Mockingbird,' to quiet her, but it didn't work. It sounded kind of silly, with the water creeping up the roof. So then she started singing 'Rock of Ages' instead. Big Daddy had a voice like a bull; after the first line he joined in. Then Mama sang it over me, and even little Jake sang along best he could, and Buglebell howled. They were all in a row, singing, and they heard, just barely heard over the flood roar and Big Daddy hammering, voices in the oak tree singing along! That was the first time they'd realized, some poor people had gotten washed into the oak and were hanging on there for dear life! They were just a couple of kids, but they were game, and they sang right along with us. Big Daddy promised to take them on the raft, even though he wasn't sure it was going to carry all of us."

"That was kind of dumb." Nan frowned.

"What was he going to do, leave them to drown? Anyway, it never came to that. Big Daddy had a friend that lived on Woodlawn Lake—only it was the West End Lake, back then—"

"Not yet," interrupted Stella. "Tell them what happened to the raft."

"Who's telling this story?" Gramma cast a withering glance at Stella and took a deep breath of smoke. "All this time, of course, things were going by on the flood. All kinds of stuff—the cloth covers they put on cars instead of roofs in those days, and chicken coops, and boards, and furniture from houses that weren't built as well as ours. And just as Big Daddy finished the raft, what should come down on the flood but somebody's stand-up piano!"

Tim's eyes went round.

"You're pulling our leg," said Nan, suspiciously.

"Lots bigger things than pianos got washed away in that flood, missy. And my mama and Big Daddy saw this one big as life bearing down on them! They were lucky it didn't smash into the roof. What it did do, though, was hit that raft dead on as it was starting to float, and broke it all to pieces!"

Nan jumped. She couldn't help it. Gramma sat back and smoked for a nerve-stretching minute before she went on.

"Now we come to Uncle Will Wright. He kept a boat

on Woodlawn Lake to go fishing in, and when he saw we were likely to have a real flood he got it ready. He and his wife had a time controlling it, but the current was taking them this way to begin with, and they managed to steer it close enough to tie onto the chimney of our house.

"There was room for all of us, but Big Daddy told them to take the kids and Polly and Mama, and then try to go rescue the folks in the tree."

"What about the dog and the cat?" asked Tim.

"They just had to take their chances with Big Daddy. Mama declared she wasn't going, either; she was going to stay with him, and she went to hand me into the boat. Just as she was leaning over the water, the current whirled the boat around, and she lost her balance. *Smack!*" Gramma slapped her knee suddenly. "There I was in the water!"

Bob piled cornstalks in an untidy heap by the garden. The birds' evening conversation was loud. Nan leaned forward.

"Soon as he saw me fall, Big Daddy dove in the water after me, but he couldn't catch me. Mama hopped on the boat, and Uncle Will cast off. We went tumbling through the water just like sticks. If the current hadn't been taking us toward the oak tree, I wouldn't be here now, and neither would any of y'all—except Bob. One of the folks in the tree leaned out and grabbed me by the blanket. Big Daddy came after, grabbed onto the trunk, and between them they hauled me in. Everybody in the tree hung on for dear

33

life till Uncle Will got his boat over and they could hand me to Polly. But as Polly took me, the tree uprooted, the boat got pushed away in the surge, and the whole lot of them in the tree went down!"

Nan twitched. Tim turned pale. Bob paused above the pile of cornstalks, bent over with his hands on his knees.

"Uncle Will's boat spun out of control, but they kept upright and made it to a rescue station. Mama was just as sure as she could be that Big Daddy was drowned, till the police rescue brought him in several hours later. They found him, fetched up against one of his own buildings that hadn't been finished yet. He and Polly went the rounds of his houses, after the water went down, and not one roof had come off, so she never did get her hundred dollars. But nobody ever saw the folks in the tree again."

"What about Buglebell and Sam?" asked Tim.

"Buglebell made it through. I kind of think Sam drowned, but we got another cat and named him Sam, too, in memory."

Bob carried the scythe back to the shed. Nan looked at the empty ditch of the creek, and at the roof of the house, seeing in her head the cold, gray water creeping up the roof above her window. "So Big Daddy was a hero," she said. "He risked his life to save you."

"He didn't think so," said Gramma. "Way he saw it, anybody would've jumped into the water after his own baby."

Bob emerged from the shed, pitchfork in one hand,

shovel in the other. Nan sucked down the sweet dregs of sugar and tea in the bottom of her glass. "I wonder why Mom never told us about that," said Tim aggrievedly. "I like floods."

"That's because you were never in one," said Stella.

"Oh, not like that. I mean stories about floods. Because of my name, you know."

Bob inserted the pitchfork under some corn stubble and pried it up. Feeling vaguely guilty, Nan put her iced-tea glass down, but kept on chewing ice. At mention of Tim's name, Gramma snorted. "Utnapishtim! What possessed Charity to give a boy such an outlandish name, I don't know!"

"I like it," said Tim. "It's not like anybody else's."

"I never saw why she couldn't just call you Noah. It's the same person, and you don't have to say it twice for people. I can't say I much like having my grandchild named out of some heathen book when he could have been named out of the Bible, either. I don't know that it isn't worse to be named after a pagan goddess, like you are, Nan, but at least Nanna sounds like a real name even when you say the whole thing."

"I thought it was smart of Aunt Charity and Uncle Simon to get names out of Babylonian literature that were family names, too," said Stella. "I always wanted a family name. 'Stella' doesn't have any history."

"There's never been a Nanna and Utnapishtim in this family before," Gramma continued.

"There's been a Nan and a Tim. Or—maybe that was a Jim? I remember playing with them."

Nan carried Bob's iced tea to him. "I can dig the rest of this all right by myself."

"Won't hurt me to finish, now I've started. Thanks." Bob took the glass and drank half of it without stopping. Nan picked up the shovel and began digging bean plants. Gramma and Stella argued amicably over whether or not any branch of the family had ever before produced a Nan or a Tim.

"Sorry to interrupt your championship of truth and justice a while ago," said Bob, "but there's no point arguing with Gramma. It makes her stubborn."

"But she's wrong!"

"Of course she is. But if she can't be wrong in her own backyard, where can she be wrong?"

They wrestled with the earth in silence for a little while. Digging was harder than it looked. "You going to be an archeologist when you grow up?" asked Bob. Satchmo sat up alertly, leaped from Tim's lap, and startled an Inca dove into the air.

She couldn't very well tell him about her plans to discover time travel, so Nan gave him the answer that would have been true last week. "I'm going to be a dean of students and live in a big house with bay windows and window seats and a tower with a weather vane on top."

"Sounds good." Bob nodded. "But don't you have to be a professor of something to get to be dean of students?"

36

"I guess so." Of all the grown-ups she'd given this answer to, he was the first to point this out. "It may as well be archeology."

"You ever been on a dig with your parents?"

"No. They're mostly interested in the Mideast. Babylon and stuff. It's too dangerous to take us, and they don't get to go very often, anyway." Something glittered among the bean roots. With a rush of excitement, Nan knelt and dug it out. It was only a green and anonymous piece of glass, but it reminded her of her duty to science. "You need to watch the dirt as you turn it over. In case of artifacts."

"I'll be careful." He knocked a handful of root against his jeans leg, watching the dirt fall, and tossed it on the growing pile of wreckage. "You know, they're doing a dig in Alamo Plaza. Maybe you should go take a look, get some idea how it's done."

"I got a book out of the library that tells all about it. But it might be nice to go look."

Tim wandered over and stood watching them with his hands in the pockets of his shorts. Nan worked a little faster, just to show off. Bob worked with method and efficiency, tearing up the plants steadily. "Tim's going to be a poet," she said, after a while, annoyed by Tim's absentminded ease. "He wants a job where you never have to sweat or get up on time."

"Everything's a trade-off," said Bob. "Poets don't ever get to live in houses with bay windows. They don't make enough money."

"I'll live with Nan," said Tim. "I can live in the tower room and stay up all night writing poetry, and in the afternoon I'll take her kids to the park."

"Fat chance," said Nan. "You can sleep in the park."

Tim's lower lip stuck out like a shelf.

"You're too much like your gramma for that," said Bob. "Blood's thicker than water, in the end."

Nan rested on her shovel, considering this. Big Daddy wouldn't have left anybody to sleep in the park. She probably would take care of Tim, when the time came, but she didn't think it would be right to let him grow up relying on that. "The end's a long way off," she said. "I guess I can pay for his funeral after he starves to death in the park."

Tim stuck his tongue out at her.

5
Tim's Find

*U*sing twine and long wire stakes from the toolshed, Nan divided the garden into five-foot-by-five-foot plots. That took a full morning, and then it was another two days before the site map she drew on graph paper looked right. "It'd be easier just to dig it all up and put stakes in where you found things," said Livvy Garza, who lived across the alley and one house down.

"That's not how it's done," said Nan, squinting at her paper as she counted squares. "You've got to scrape all the dirt away and keep track of how deep everything you find is. You'll get all confused about what was where if you don't have a map."

"It looks like a pain in the neck to me," said Livvy.

Gramma was picking half-ripe tomatoes on the edge of the creek. "Nan's not the sort to mind that," she piped up. "Taking pains runs in the family. My daddy never used to let go of a job till it was finished, come hell or high water."

"Was he an archeologist, too?"

"No. He was a builder. He was the one built this whole neighborhood, back when I was a little girl."

"Wow," said Livvy. "My house, too?"

"That's right. When the depression came on, hardly anybody could afford houses, but he kept right on doing little jobs, and bought up land however he could, and it paid off for him after the war."

A glow of pride warmed Nan's stomach. It was this glow that kept her digging in square number 5N4E, where she had found the pipe, for three fruitless days. Each morning, after washing the breakfast dishes, she donned sunscreen, gimme cap, and work gloves, kneeling on the battered rubber cushion Grampa had used for weeding. It was hotter than she had ever thought mornings could be. Her sides, back, and arms ached from loosening the dirt with a trowel, dragging it out with the cut-off bottom of a plastic milk jug, and sifting it through an old sieve. All she found were rocks, old seed packets, and a few Popsicle sticks. Ants crawled over her toes, and mosquitoes tormented her bare arms, while Gramma bustled in and out on apparently endless housecleaning errands, and Tim read ancient Hardy Boys books under the pecan tree.

"You could do some of this, too, you know," she said one morning, when he got up to carry in the book he had just finished and get another one. "Or don't you want to be rich?"

"You're not going to get rich like that," said Tim. "It's magic, not science, and it'll work when it wants to. Otherwise we would've been able to go see Grampa by now."

"Not if it's one of the rules that you can only use each artifact for one time-trip." Nan had thought of this a couple of days ago and had written it down in the back of her spiral notebook as a hypothesis that had to be proved or disproved. "Maybe there's some kind of energy that stores up, and it's just enough to get you out and back. We have to find something else before we can draw any conclusions."

"You're not going to find anything good there, anyway. Gramma said the garden'd be good because of the creek washing stuff up. I bet the creek hasn't been over here since the night Gramma almost drowned. You have to dig right on the bank, if you want to find anything."

This sounded so much like sense that Nan immediately got cranky. "Why don't you dig up the bank, then, smarty?"

"Because it won't do any good. The magic'll happen just the same whether we kill ourselves digging up the yard or not."

"You're just scared," declared Nan. "You don't really want to time travel. You're scared you'll get stuck."

Tim turned red. "I am not! You're just mad because you can't find anything and you know I could."

"You could not. You don't know where to dig any better than I do."

"I do so." Grim-faced, Tim took the trowel and picked his way across the garden to square 1S6E, where he began hacking at the creek bank.

"That's not in the garden," Nan objected. "Gramma said we couldn't dig up the whole yard."

"If you didn't want to dig here you shouldn't've staked it," said Tim defiantly.

At least she was no longer the only one working, but she'd brought out only the one trowel. And Tim had left his book on the grass. If he was going to keep reading Gramma's books, he needed to be more careful with them. Nan wiped her hands on her shorts before carrying the book back inside. She had barely returned to her place, armed with the other trowel, when Tim squealed.

"Hey! I found something!"

"What?" snapped Nan. "A bottle cap?"

"No. I can't tell what it is. Just a minute while I get it all the way out!"

"Stop poking at it! You might break it." Nan scooped up the equipment she had gathered but had had no occasion to use yet—the sandwich bags, the tweezers, the paint-brushes, and the clipboard of graph paper, just begging to have finds recorded on it. "It's probably just a rock, anyway," she said, finding him tugging at a whitish object in a tangle of fine grass roots. "You're doing this all wrong. Go get the pruning shears out of the shed." She shouldered him aside and brushed dirt away with a watercolor brush. This was not a rock.

Her care in removing the object was increased by Tim's impatience. She clipped the roots, brushed the dirt off, and even made what her library book called an *"in situ* drawing,"* showing it exactly as they had found it. By the time she let him pick it up, his excitement was out of all proportion to the thing's appearance. "What d'you think it is?" he demanded eagerly.

Nan waited for him to pass it to her and then examined it with her best superior air. It was roughly cube shaped and had been white, once, with a layer of worn black plastic on one short side, and four holes in the other. She picked at the black plastic, and recognition struck. "It's a shoe heel, of course," she said. "Kind of a clunky shoe."

Tim's face fell. "But that's boring!"

Nan's own disappointment was lessened by her satisfaction that Tim's first, effortless find was so much less impressive than her own had been. "Mom and Dad get all excited about broken dishes," she said, wrapping the find in a sandwich bag and labeling it.

"Yeah, but they find dishes older than Jesus."

"This is probably older than we are. People don't wear big heels like this now. Maybe it's from World War II." She gave him the clipboard. "Here. Each of these squares is six inches, and this X shows where the heel was. Make sure you mark down the next thing you find in relation to it."

"You really think it could be from World War II?" asked Tim. "You think maybe it's off one of Gramma's nurse shoes?"

"I don't think nurses ever wore heels, but maybe. We can ask her when we go in."

Tim returned happily to his demolition of the creek bank. Nan took a walk around the site, stepping carefully over the twine borders and studying the ground. She was going to have to pick a better place. It would be copying to switch to a square directly on the bank, though. Uncertain just what she was looking for, she went from square to square, occasionally poking her trowel into the dry, hard ground. Nan began to sing.

"Fish heads, fish heads, roly-poly fish heads.
Fish heads, fish heads, eat 'em up, yum!"

Test holes. That was what she needed. A small, straight hole, one in each square, to get a sample of what might be in each. It wasn't a fun prospect. The broad hole she'd already dug had a tendency to collapse in on the sides, and this would be worse in a smaller shaft. Gramma had not been watering the yard, because she said there was a drought on and it was their duty to conserve water, but if Nan could get permission to water the garden the night before—

"That's the stupidest song in the whole world," said

44

Tim. "I bet you couldn't make any song dumber than that if you tried."

"Mom says you can do anything if you try hard enough." Nan sat back on her heels and rocked back and forth, thinking.

> "Shoe heel, shoe heel, Timmy found a shoe heel.
> Shoe heel, shoe heel, where's it from?"

"My name's not Timmy!"

Nan ignored him and resang the chorus, groping for a suitably worthless verse. She found it by forcing the emphasis firmly down onto the wrong syllables.

> "Can't be a nurse's; it's too high for that.
> Wasn't very well made; maybe was a bum's."

"Okay, that's stupider than 'Fish Heads,' " Tim conceded, hacking at the ground with the edge of his trowel. "It can't be a bum's. White shoes are always good shoes." He paused with the trowel in midair, and waved it like a conductor:

> "Used to be white so it used to be fancy,
> Till it came off at a party and the owner felt dumb.
> Shoe heel, shoe heel, I just found a shoe heel.
> Shoe heel, shoe heel, where's it from?"

45

Struck by a thought, Nan scrambled to retrieve the heel from its bag. "Hey, we got an artifact, we got a poem! Experiment time!"

"That's not a poem," protested Tim.

Nan plunked down on the bank just above him. "So if it doesn't work we'll have to make a real one. Come on, now. Shoe heel, shoe heel . . ."

Tim joined in reluctantly. Nan closed her eyes, mouthing the words around a shivering anticipation. Tim was probably right. The song was probably too silly for the purpose. But gravity worked just as well on broken Mickey Mouse balloons as it did on damaged 747s. "Shoe heel, shoe heel, where's it from?" she sang, for the third time, and felt a ripple creep from her scalp to her soles.

She and Tim fell silent at the same time. The air had cooled abruptly, and a babble of sound clicked on like a radio—grown-up voices, a child calling his mom, a dog barking. The smell of barbecue, borne on a pleasant breeze, tickled Nan's nose.

Holding her breath, Nan opened her eyes and turned her head.

At once she realized that she was hopelessly underdressed.

6
Warm Reception

Although the sun was almost directly overhead, all the people standing in small groups around the yard were dressed up—men and boys in suits, and many of the women and girls in long dresses. Gramma, wrapped in an enormous apron and clouds of smoke, basted an array of meat, on a grill made from a steel drum, with barbecue sauce. A long table had been set up near the honeysuckle-brilliant back fence, and on it towered a wedding cake as tall as Tim.

"Criminently," breathed Tim, cowering below the bank. "What's going on?"

At that moment, a pair of familiar figures appeared on the back porch. Nan would have known them anywhere, even at this distance, even without the picture in the living room. Someone called out: "There they are! Three cheers for the bride and groom!" Grampa's camera flashed as the

47

cheer went up. "Come up, you idiot!" hissed Nan. "We did it! We're at Mom and Dad's wedding!"

She was afraid he'd drag them back to their own time before they'd had a chance to look around again; but he scrambled up beside her, his eyes round as quarters. The grown-ups crowded around Mom and Dad, and the kids hovered near the wedding cake. It was a good thing Mom had changed out of her gown and veil already, because everyone seemed determined to pass her from hand to hand for kisses, like a baby, and any white lace and satin would have been shredded. Nan and Tim, conspicuous in their cutoffs, approached the other children.

"This is so-o-o boring," sighed one boy, twisting around on one heel.

"I'm hungry!" whined a dark-haired little girl, in a narrow dotted-swiss skirt that reached to the tops of her shoes.

"Oh, shut up. She's on her way to cut the cake right now," ordered a boy slightly younger than Tim. "You can eat then."

"But I'm hungry now!"

"C'mon, Stella," said an older girl, helpfully. "Stand by me, and you'll be in the picture when the cake's cut."

Nan stared. Stella? That was Stella? She couldn't be more than six! Suddenly Nan felt dizzy.

"Hey!" The bored boy stopped twisting and glared accusingly at them. Tim slid behind Nan, leaving her to bear the brunt of his stare. "Who're you?"

"How come y'all get to wear shorts?" demanded the boy who'd told Stella to shut up. (That must be Cousin Mike, Stella's big brother, who had joined the Air Force and was currently in Greenland.)

"I guess our folks had more sense than yours did," retorted Nan, unthinkingly. "They didn't want us getting barbecue sauce on our good clothes."

"I didn't see you in church," objected the oldest girl. Stella hung on her hand and gazed at them grimly.

"Oh, we had our good clothes on then. We brought these in the car and changed when we got here."

Before Nan had to field any more questions, Mom and Dad and a horde of grown-ups descended on the refreshment table, scattering the group of children. Nan and Tim retreated, trying to stay out of the way of Grampa's camera as he fussed over each step in the cake cutting. As they lurked under the fig tree, Tim said into her ear: "This is weird. Mom looked straight at me just now, and she didn't know me!"

"Don't worry about it," Nan whispered back. "They won't be Mom and Dad for years, remember?"

"That doesn't help!"

The cake was cut and distributed at last, and Gramma began dishing ribs and beef slices onto fancy paper plates. The yard became social and relaxed. Nan, hungered by the smell, sneaked some barbecue off the corner of the buffet. Tim filled Stella's plate for her and wandered off between her and the oldest girl. Nan got into a contest

49

with a couple of boys (Who were all these people?) as to who could eat the most barbecue in five minutes. She wished she were brave enough to approach Grampa—not that she was scared, really, but he was so busy eating, and taking pictures, and talking to people—and of course he wouldn't know who she was. That thought made her skin crawl. She distracted herself by counting up people she knew.

Aunt Marian looked young and cranky in the second-nicest dress there. Gramma's little brother, Great-Uncle Ben, had a surprising amount of hair. Stella's mother, Aunt Faith, was almost as busy as Gramma, her face unlined and her hair the color of coffee. Aunt Hope wore love beads over her lacy Mexican blouse, and looked all set for her commune in California, though Nan knew she hadn't moved there till after Mom moved north. Grandma and Grandad Bragg, Dad's parents, were a little too well dressed, and Nan was not tempted to approach them. She loved them, of course, but she didn't really like them as much as she did Gramma and Grampa. Even with paper plates in their hands, they looked stiff and formal, their suits a little darker than anyone else's, and whoever she happened to see them talking to always looked as if he wanted to talk to someone else.

A howl from Stella split the babble of conversation. Nan dashed to the back fence, where Stella sat bawling amid a puddle of punch at which Tim dabbed hopelessly with a paper napkin. Mike got there first, and pounced on Tim. "What'd you do to her?"

"Nothing." Tim pointed at the honeysuckle, just as a black tail pulled into the leaves. "The cat scratched her. I told her it wouldn't like being picked up by the scruff."

Nan looked at the arm Stella was holding as a cluster of aunts hurried up, slowed by their high heels. The scratch had drawn blood, but wasn't very long. "We'd better put something on it." Stella jerked loose from her and continued crying with the unselfconscious abandon of the very small.

"Let me see it, honey," crooned Aunt Faith, scooping Stella up and bearing her off to the house without bothering to listen to Tim's explanation. Aunt Marian looked down her nose at them exactly as she did at Jehovah's Witnesses. "This isn't a neighborhood party, kids," she said sternly.

"It's all right, ma'am," said the oldest girl. "They're invited."

"Oh? They're not dressed for it."

"Our folks didn't want us getting barbecue on our good clothes," explained Nan, stung. That was no way to look at your own niece, whether you knew who she was or not!

"Oh, yes, the barbecue!" said Aunt Marian darkly. "And where are your folks?"

"Now, mellow out," said Aunt Hope. "You're way too uptight today. Even if they are gate-crashers, what's the diff?"

"We're not gate-crashers!" protested Tim. "We belong here!"

"Oh? Which side of the family are you on?"

Aunt Marian's voice and expression were like a cold slap. Tim opened his mouth and closed it again. Nan scrambled through her brain for a plausible lie, but suddenly Gramma came bustling to the rescue.

"They're some kind of Chadwells," she said, barely glancing at them as she bore down on Aunt Marian with a platter in one hand and a greasy spatula in the other. "Little girl's got my own daddy's face on. Don't y'all pay her any mind, now!" The hairs on Nan's arms rose when Gramma looked straight at her—a dark-haired Gramma, in unfamiliar glasses—with no spark of recognition. "This is Marian Bragg, the groom's sister, and she keeps forgetting"—with a hard and meaningful look!—"that it's the bride's family arranges the wedding!"

Aunt Marian turned with sudden ferocity. "All I ever did was make a few suggestions!"

She did not stop there, but all the children slipped away with one accord. "What's that about?" asked Nan, around a lump of embarrassment in her throat.

"Oh, the groom's family kept butting in on the wedding plans," said the oldest girl. "You know what Nomi's like!" Nomi? Oh, various cousins used that name for Gramma —it was easier to say than "Great-Aunt Naomi." Nan remembered this without missing anything the girl said.

52

"My mom says we wouldn't be having barbecue if Mrs. Bragg hadn't waltzed in talking about a formal reception."

Nan looked over her shoulder. Gramma and Aunt Marian were still at it. People had begun to edge away from the area, leaving an empty circle in the middle of which they began to raise their voices—not loud enough, yet, to be understood.

"Gramma shouldn't be yelling at her," said Tim critically, but without heat. Nan could tell by the droop of his mouth that Aunt Marian's treatment of him still stung.

"Aunt Marian shouldn't be butting in, either," said Nan, absently. She couldn't see Mom and Dad anywhere.

Aunt Marian turned on her heel and stalked toward the refreshment table. Nan was relaxing when her aunt lurched to a stop, balancing on one foot like a graceless ballerina. One white-sandaled foot waved in the air above a small piece of white.

Gramma laughed. "Sorry, Marian! Didn't mean to make you fall apart!"

Aunt Marian shot her a black look, squatted unsteadily, and picked up the clunky white heel. She wobbled again fitting it back on, stamped twice, and continued on her way with an unnaturally stiff back.

"It'll never stay on," said Nan, feeling the uncomfortable bulk of the heel in her pocket.

"She should've made up, just then," said the oldest girl. "If she'd laughed back, Nomi would've been all right."

"She probably thought Gramma was laughing at her to be mean," said Tim.

"Nomi isn't like that," said the oldest girl absently, waving at somebody. "'Scuse me a minute, y'all."

Left alone with her brother, Nan turned to him. "You ready to go?"

"I thought you were all het up to talk to Grampa."

Grampa was over by the back porch talking to Grandad Bragg. Nan looked at them and looked away. "He wouldn't know us."

"He'd be nice to us, anyway."

"But what would we talk about?"

To Nan's relief, Tim had no answer. They went in search of a private place to vanish from, but the yard was crawling with people. Maybe they would be less conspicuous inside—but to get in the back door they'd have to walk right past their grandfathers. They circled around the side, to go in at the front.

Fortunately, they saw their parents before their parents saw them.

7
Rescue Mission

"—my mom's fault as much as your sister's," Mom was saying, slumping wearily under the pecan tree. "I wish we could just walk off and leave the whole bunch to their own devices!"

"Well—why not?" asked Dad. "All we need is your suitcase."

"As soon as they saw me ready to leave they'd be on us like a swarm of locusts." Nan knew by the movement of her mother's arm and head that she was rubbing at a headache between her eyes. "I'm really not up to telling my whole family I'm sick of them right now."

Nan recognized the tone, the stance, the futile attempt to erase a headache. Something had driven Mom to the end of her rope, and if Dad—or somebody—didn't do something soon, she would start to snap at everybody, temporarily bereft of all patience and good temper. It had something to do with the sugar in her blood. Dad looked around, as if hoping for a genie to spring out of the ground, and spotted Nan and Tim.

It was terrible to see him smile nervously, as if at strangers. "Uh—hi, kids," he said. "Don't think I've met you two."

Tim stood with his mouth open, looking fragile. Nan reached out to take control of the situation. "Um—we could go get her suitcase for you."

"Were you listening?" Mom demanded.

"Not on purpose!" burst out Tim. "We didn't do anything! Mom—"

He was about to say something stupid! Nan cut him off. "We're sorry. We couldn't help it. I could go get your suitcase for you and we wouldn't tell anybody you'd left. Cross my heart."

"Right. You're going to just waltz up to my room and out again with my suitcase without anybody noticing." Another minute and Mom would lose her temper. "Oh, why didn't we elope?"

Nan gave Tim a push. "Go get the twine Grampa keeps behind the shed door."

Tim glared at her. "You ain't the boss of me!"

"Just do it!" She didn't wait to watch him obey, but turned back to Mom and Dad. "I can climb the tree and lower your suitcase on a line. It's that window there, right?"

"Yes." Mom looked up doubtfully. "Are you sure—?"

"I've done it before."

"What about the screen?" asked Dad, in his let's-be-practical voice.

"There isn't—" Yes, there was. Her window now had the same top-hinged wooden screen as all the others—and, Nan realized with a qualm, the pecan tree was smaller than it had been. Concentrate on the screen. It didn't fit flush to the wall, but stuck out a little, like the one in Tim's room that had lost its hook. "It's not fastened at the bottom," she pointed out. "It'll work fine."

"Look, this isn't important enough to risk your neck for," said Mom.

"I've told you, I've done it before." Nan looked at her steadily. "You shouldn't have to fight your way out of your own wedding."

Mom studied her face for a minute. "I'm supposed to know you, aren't I? I'm sorry. I'm real bad at keeping track of the family."

Nan felt hot all over. "It's because I look like Big Daddy," she said. "Don't worry about it. How many suitcases are there?"

Mom laughed shakily. "Yep, you're a Chadwell all right! All business! There's just the one small one left, packed and on the foot of the bed. Everything else was put in the car this morning. Are you one of Aunt Becky's horde? I never can keep track of the New Mexico branch."

Tim's return prevented Nan's having to answer. He thrust a full plate at Mom. "Here. You never ate anything but wedding cake. That's how come you're so cranky."

"What is this, my day to be baby-sat?"

"He's right, you know," said Dad. "You eat and we'll take care of this."

Mom looked at the ribs, potato salad, corn bread, and Jell-O on the plate with distaste but began eating doggedly. Nan made sure her T-shirt was tucked securely into her shorts, and dropped the twine down her front. Dad bent over and made his hands into a stirrup.

This boost got her a higher start than the one Tim had given her, and the tree was over fifteen years smaller, so the first part of the climbing was a breeze. She was only halfway up when she heard a *woop* of breath and felt the tree shake slightly as Dad came up after her. "I can do it myself," she said.

"No doubt," said Dad. When he smiled at her, she could see where the lines on his face were going to be. "I'm just standing by in case."

Nan would never have asked him to come up, but now he was behind her, the distance to the window was less intimidating. Nonetheless, it was only with a grim gathering of resolution that she made the long step to the roof, clinging to the windowsill and scrambling breathlessly for a moment before she found a foothold on the shingle. "You okay?" asked Mom anxiously.

"No problem," said Nan, taking a couple of steadying

breaths. The slope of the roof was not steep, and her tennis shoes gripped the asbestos well. She took one hand from the windowsill and hoisted the screen.

She had to duck under her arm and sideways to get out of its way, a maneuver that surprised the muscles of her upper arm with a stab of pain. She snorted with the effort and suddenly felt the weight removed. Dad had leaned out uncomfortably along the roof, clinging to the branch with his knees, and taken the screen. "Go on," he said, "I've got it."

Nan went through the window less clumsily than she had last time, and the screen banged shut behind her. Faintly, she could hear Mom say, "Why am I putting y'all through this?"

"We may as well go on now we're this far," Dad called down.

"Rats! I hoped I'd be the first one to remember the upstairs bathroom!" said someone just outside the door.

"You'll just have to wait your turn like the rest of us," answered someone else.

"Shh!" hissed Nan out the window. "There's people in the hall up here!"

The room and furniture were the same as she had woken to that morning, but the books on the shelves were college textbooks and mystery novels, not Nancy Drew and the Little Colonel. Pictures were fewer and differently arranged. It had a young-lady smell, lipstick-kissed Kleenex in the wastebasket, and a *Redbook* magazine on the bedside table. The wedding dress hung neatly on the back of the door, waiting for Gramma to clean it and pack it away in the cedar chest—where, one rainy day far to the north, Nan would find it, and Mom would struggle into it, laughing.

Nan untucked her shirt and let the twine fall out. The suitcase at the foot of the bed was the same one Nan had packed her socks and underwear in to come to Gramma's, only much newer. The plastic tag hanging from the zipper bore the name Charity Bragg in proud gold letters. Nan locked it conscientiously, and tied the twine to the handle in the best knot she could remember from Girl Scouts. When she hoisted it to the windowsill, Dad swung himself across the roof again and took it from her while she held the screen up. "Look out below!" called Dad softly, lowering it through the young-leaved branches.

Footsteps and voices passed up and down the stairs and the hallway as Nan waited.

"How goes the feud?"

"Our team's winning."

"Of course! We outnumber them!"

"Miss Marian's lost her shoe for good and she fell in the creek chasing a napkin."

"Serve her right, the little snot."

Nan took a step toward the door before she remembered she was in hiding.

"Oh, be fair, now. There wouldn't be any fight if it wasn't for Naomi."

60

"She's just defending her own turf."

Nan remembered suddenly that she had not written to Aunt Marian since they came to Texas. She ought to do that. Dad dropped the end of the twine and signaled her to come out. She opened the screen with her hands and head. Dad held it long enough for her to clamber out onto the roof, but before she got through, the screen shifted suddenly, one corner coming down on her heel and making her jump. The screen banged against the window frame as Dad dropped it and grabbed her. She only slid a few inches, but she found she had grabbed him back, and her heart thumped furiously. Below, Tim and Mom both cried out.

Dad steadied himself with one hand on the roof. "You okay?"

She nodded. "Somebody will've heard that. Let's get down!"

When they achieved the ground, Mom hugged Dad awkwardly around her plate. "What was that about?"

"One of the hinges broke," said Dad. "We need to make our getaway fast."

Mom laughed, the suitcase in her hand, as they proceeded to the front of the house. "This isn't what I figured our wedding would be like, y'all! Now, let's just hope nobody's hanging out around the cars."

Nobody was, though a neighbor waved from across the street. Cars lined both sides of the block, but Nan knew which one was Mom and Dad's right away. It was a brown two-door, with slogans sprayed all over it: JUST MARRIED. LOVEBIRDS R US. CAUTION: NERVOUS GROOM DRIVING.

"We better get going before somebody looks out a window," said Mom, sounding stable and calm. She looked down at Nan and Tim. "Thanks, y'all. If I ever get around to having kids, I'll see what I can do to make them as nice and helpful as you."

"I'm sure you'll do fine," said Nan solemnly.

For a minute she thought Mom was going to hug her, and she didn't know if she wanted that or not; then Dad opened the car door for her. Tim, who'd been looking thoughtful all this while, suddenly cried, "Oh! There's nobody to throw the old shoe!"

Nan took off her tennis shoe and handed it to him. "This old enough?"

They waved as Dad turned the car around and drove away. Mom twisted around in her shoulder harness to wave back. Tim hurled the shoe with all his might. Nan hopped into the street to retrieve it when the car rounded the corner. "We better get on home," she said, jamming on her shoe. "We don't know how long we've been gone back in our time."

"What if we can't get home?" asked Tim. "I don't know how it happened last time."

"We'll get there all right," said Nan stoutly, though she wasn't sure how. The solution to another problem had occurred to her, though. "Let's go in the creek. Nobody'll see us there."

62

They climbed over the guard rail and clambered all the way to the bottom. The grass was thick and green here, studded with bluebonnets and pink and white flowers like scattered tissue paper. "You suppose we should click our heels together three times and say, 'There's no place like home'?" asked Tim.

"It can't hurt." Nan took his hand and closed her eyes.

It's not working, she thought, the third time they said it, with a catch of fear in her heart. Then the ripple started, working from top to bottom, and Tim's grip on her hand tightened. The air grew hot and still around her, less sweet smelling. The birdsong she had stopped hearing thinned out noticeably. Nan opened her eyes. The bluebonnets and pink flowers had been replaced by straggling forget-me-nots, and the grass was higher. Her shadow lay small beneath her. Up at the house, Gramma was calling them to lunch.

Lunch! thought Nan. How can I possibly eat lunch after all that barbecue?

8
Drought

*N*an spent the next morning digging test holes. The best thing she turned up was charcoal and ash about three inches down in square number 4N5E. According to the book she kept checking out of the library, this meant that Indians had lived here once. Excited, Nan, Tim, and Livvy spent most of a week digging in and around 4N5E; but, instead of arrowheads, they found a puzzling assortment of more modern items. Nan set up a card table on the back porch to sort them.

"This book just isn't any good for this kind of site," grumbled Nan, leaning it against the table leg. "It shows you all different types of arrowheads and things, but it doesn't say word one about dolls and plastic."

"We could get books that did," said Livvy, spreading tiny shards of scorched pottery on an old towel.

"It'll be easier to ask Gramma," said Tim, putting down a lump of plastic to rap on the kitchen windowsill.

"Gra-amma!"

Her face appeared over the row of ripening figs and tomatoes. "What's up? Lunch is almost ready."

"Can you help us identify artifacts?" asked Nan. "We're stumped."

"Just a minute. Let me stir the soup." She soon emerged through the back door. "Goodness, y'all've been working hard!" She had been too busy making bridesmaid dresses for the daughter of a friend of Aunt Faith's to look at their finds yet this week. When she saw the array of small, broken dishes, charred wood, and twisted pieces of metal, her smile faded. "Oh, my," she said softly. "I never even thought about that!"

"Never thought about what?" asked Nan.

Livvy stood up and offered Gramma her chair. Gramma sank into it and lit a cigarette absently, her eyes coming to rest on the doll in front of Nan. It was a tiny, inconvenient doll, naked and impossible to dress, with its legs touching each other and its arms molded against the body. Nan wasn't sure what it was made of—something like china, only less smooth. Gramma picked her up and looked over the cracked, blackened figure sadly.

"Never thought about what?" Nan persisted.

"I ought to take the fifth on that," said Gramma, blowing smoke out through her nose. "I don't like to think I was ever that naughty!"

"It's too late to change," Tim pointed out. "And now you've gotten us all curious."

"What are these things?" asked Nan.

"Well—this is what you call a penny doll. And that's my Betty Boop doll's dinner service. It's hard to tell about the rest." She picked up the blob of melted plastic, and laid it down again. "My Orphan Annie shaker mug—I had been so proud of that. They were supposed to be free, but of course you had to collect box tops, and use postage, so a lot of girls just made their own, but I had the real thing."

"But how did they get all burned up?" asked Livvy. "Did your brothers do it to you?" She had four brothers, two on each side, and never hesitated to blame them for anything.

"No. No, I did this to myself."

Tim squeaked. Nan looked from the blackened remains to Gramma's face. "Why on earth would you burn your own toys?"

"I was mad," said Gramma ruefully. "I don't think I've ever been that mad, before or since."

"Mad at who?" asked Tim.

"And what about?" asked Nan.

"And why take it out on your own toys?" asked Livvy.

"I barely remember." Gramma tapped ash loose against the edge of the table, and stepped on the lump that fell to the floor. "It was so long ago—over fifty years, think of that! It was something to do—I felt like I was a grown-

66

up and Mama treated me like a baby. I must've been about Nan's age, give or take. It was Halloween, and everybody'd gone off somewhere without me, and I was burning mad, so I made a bonfire of all my old toys—well, not all. I've still got a couple of dolls, and that dollhouse, that I saved so my kids could play with them. All the ordinary cheap stuff went up in smoke, though. It was to show I was a grown-up, because grown-ups aren't attached to toys. I never thought till afterward that it was a childish thing to do." She drew a long drag on the cigarette, the column of ash creeping closer to her mouth. "Was that the same night I went on a rampage with that little girl from the Hooverville? I remember her popping up out of the dark back of a bonfire like a ghost, and we didn't have bonfires all that often. Maybe she was a ghost—I never did see her in school, and I looked."

Nan saw Tim's eyes go wide, and knew he was going to be silly about ghosts. "You couldn't expect her to go to your school if she lived in Hooverville," she said.

A laugh routed the sadness from Gramma's face. "Hoovervilles couldn't afford their own schools, honey. That's what we called a shantytown back then, when everybody was blaming President Hoover for the depression. People that'd lost their homes would build shelters on the edge of town out of whatever they could find."

"Oh. Like homeless people living in cardboard boxes."

"Just like tha—Satchmo! No!"

No one had noticed the cat approaching till he jumped

into the middle of the artifacts and made room for himself. By the time they'd chased him off and straightened the table, the soup was ready (incredibly good soup, made of chicken stock and maverick tomatoes, that made Nan vow never to open a can again), and they all went in to lunch.

It was a good thing they finished excavating the bonfire when they did. That same night, Gramma looked at the thermometer when it came to be Tim's bedtime, and said, "Way too hot to sleep inside." She produced cots from the closet in the sewing room—once Aunt Faith's bedroom —and set them up on the back porch. The next morning was too hot to consider digging, so Nan decided they should conduct experiments instead. She set Tim to making poetry while she and Livvy watched movies on Livvy's mother's VCR, in air-conditioned comfort.

Except for a flurry of rain on the Fourth of July—not enough to spoil the fireworks at Fort Sam Houston—the days were long and ovenlike. Tim went around chanting the shortest poem he had ever made:

> "Too hot to run,
> Too hot to play,
> Too hot to do anything today!"

Gramma made them take baths instead of showers, and all the moisture the yard got was waste water left over from soaking dirty pans. "The aquifer is sinking a foot a day!" she would exclaim, if she caught Nan letting the water run while brushing her teeth. "Isn't that fast enough for you?" Apparently, the aquifer was the only water source in San Antonio, and when it dried up, there just wouldn't be any more.

They were supposed to go to the Sea World of Texas on Nan's twelfth birthday, but just as they were walking out the door, Gramma sat down hard on the top step, gasping for breath. Her skin was suddenly grayish and clammy where Nan touched her. For a moment Nan was too terrified to move; then Gramma fished in her pocket for her pillbox, and Nan ran to fetch cold water. Gramma didn't speak till she had drunk it all, and her face had returned to a more nearly normal color. "Oh, dear!" She mopped her face with the monogrammed handkerchief Tim had given her for her last birthday. "I'm sorry, honey! I don't think I'd be much fun at Sea World today!"

Nan swallowed her disappointment. "That's okay. We don't have to go."

Gramma shook her head. "Fiddlesticks! You might have to wait and get Stella and Bob to take you, that's all."

"Don't you think you could feel better tomorrow?" asked Tim, anxiously. Livvy had told him Sea World had a pool full of dolphins you could pet, and he hadn't talked about anything else for two days. Nan was ashamed of him and answered before Gramma could do more than shake her head and smile thinly.

"Saturday's plenty soon enough," she declared. "We can invite Livvy and her brothers over for the cake this afternoon, and I'll go to the mall with my birthday money."

They shut up the living room and turned on the airconditioning so Gramma could rest—though she said she felt silly, lying down in the middle of the morning. Nan and Tim stayed outside, so as not to disturb her, and Nan made sandwiches for lunch.

They continued their experiments while waiting to go to Sea World, but they were getting discouraged. Tim would make a poem about one of the bonfire artifacts, and they would try saying it in different parts of the yard, on the porch, in the creek, in one or the other bedroom; and nothing would happen. Nan had started collecting other things to experiment on—one of Grampa's pictures, an old shoe she picked up at the traffic light by the Presbyterian church, or a broken toy salvaged from the alley; but none of them worked, either. She got tired of writing out descriptions of similar experiments and noting "No Result" next to all of them. "I think there's something wrong with your poems," she told Tim.

"My poems are just fine!" Tim protested. "Anyway, it's not easy making poems about broken dishes."

"You're not putting your mind to it." Nan flipped through the notebook and found the one he'd written for the penny doll, reading it aloud in an exaggerated, prissy voice:

70

"When Gramma was a little girl
She bought a penny doll
From a wizened, toothless lady
that kept a market stall—

Now that's not even true. Gramma says you bought penny dolls at the five-and-dime."

"That's boring. Anyway, you couldn't do any better."

"I didn't say I could. I said you needed to."

"I don't think it's my poetry that's the matter. I think it's those stupid artifacts. They haven't got any significance." He brought out each syllable of this last word with evident satisfaction.

"They're just as significant as Aunt Marian's heel," Nan retorted.

"And my poems are all better than that shoe heel song!" Tim stomped out the back door, calling for Satchmo. He hadn't made friends with any of the neighborhood boys, but all the cats in the neighborhood just loved him. Well, they could have him! Nan got her swimsuit and ran across the alley to see if Livvy wanted to go to the Y.

Bob and Stella got them to Sea World Saturday morning in time to get good seats for the first killer whale show. Nan was glad she had waited. Gramma would have had a hard time with all the walking that proved necessary in order to see everything. Also, she wouldn't have let them sit where they could get wet; or, if she had, would not have enjoyed it the way Stella and Bob did. Nan spent what was left of the birthday money getting the biggest, prettiest conch shell she could find for Aunt Marian.

Fighting off exhaustion, they stayed for the closing fireworks, and joined the crowd tramping, sore-footed and silent, across the vast parking lot. Tim was asleep before they got back to the highway. Stella laid her head back and sighed. "I'm glad Gramma didn't come! That would've half killed her!"

Nan thought about this, watching the shapes of trees loom in and out of sight as the line of cars crawled past. She remembered how gray and clammy Gramma had been for a couple of minutes and felt a little clammy inside herself. "Do you mean for real?" she asked. "Like Grampa?"

"Dadgum," said Stella. "I forgot about little pitchers."

"Twelve's not so little. And Tim's asleep already."

"It's not anything you have to worry about," said Bob. "Probably she'll be fine for several years yet. But she is getting on, and she eats too much, and she smokes too much, and she can't do as much as she used to. That's just a fact of life."

"I keep telling her not to smoke."

Stella laughed. "So does Bob! I'm afraid you're both way too late on that one."

" 'You may think you know what's best for everybody, Mr. Med Student, but that don't mean everybody's going to agree with you,' " said Bob, in a voice clearly meant to mimic Gramma. " 'I was a nurse decades before you was a gleam in your daddy's eye!' "

Nan blinked at the itch under her contacts. "We ought to all get together and make her stop."

"You can't go around making people do things," said Stella.

"Why not? We're right, and she's wrong!"

"That's not always the important consideration," said Bob, finally getting onto the highway and speeding up.

The night was so hot that, even lying on top of the sheets on the cot on the back porch, Nan felt as if she were being smothered in steamed towels. Her legs ached. Her sore feet had been white and puffy when she took her shoes off. Despite her exhaustion, she heard the chiming clock sound midnight faintly through the open windows before she slept.

9
Heated Moments

*T*he cool dawn breeze woke Nan, sticky from the night's heat. Satchmo balanced on the porch rail, staring at the fig tree. The figs they had picked the previous morning would be completely ripe by now. Nan thought, I'll get up and pick some more and clean yesterday's so we can have them for breakfast. Even Gramma won't want a hot breakfast today.

Her thighs were damper than the rest of her; she must've slept with her legs crossed. She rolled over, tugging her nightgown loose from her sticky skin, and noticed the big reddish-brown patches on the sheet.

Nan's heart stood still. She fumbled for her glasses, hooked over the frame of the cot. Oh, no. There was blood on her sheets, and the back of her nightgown, and—she checked—on the insides of her thighs. Lots of blood. She was hemorrhaging. Visions of hospitals, transfusions, and

74

feeding tubes flashed through her brain. She mustn't panic. She didn't feel any pain. Probably there was time for the doctors to save her.

Gramma was asleep on her back with her mouth open and her arms folded regally. Nan shook her, gently at first, then harder. "Gramma! Gramma, wake up! It's an emergency!"

Gramma's eyes fluttered, and she goggled blindly. "Charity?"

Nan shook her emphatically. "Wake up! I'm hemorrhaging! You've got to take me to the hospital."

Gramma sat up and shoved her glasses onto her nose, eyes suddenly clear and sharp. "What?"

Nan turned half around and pulled out the skirt of her nightgown. "See?"

To her astonishment, Gramma laughed. "Oh, honey! You must still be half asleep. That's not real blood."

Nan blinked. "But—then what is it?"

"Honestly, I thought they taught this stuff in school these days! It's just the time of the month."

"The what?" Nan's panic ebbed before the uncomfortable certainty that she was about to feel stupid.

"The time of the month. The curse. You're becoming a woman, that's all."

Nan looked down at the red patches, enlightenment dawning. "You mean I started my period?"

"Of course you did. I'm ashamed of your mom! She should've prepared you better."

"She talked to me about it." Nan's face burned. "And we had it in school. I just—we never—look, nobody told me I was going to bleed like a stuck pig, okay?"

Gramma laughed again. "What did you think was going to happen?"

"Well—I—I guess I just didn't think about it."

Gramma's feet fumbled under the cot for her slippers. "Well, you go get cleaned up, and I'll run out and get you some Kotex. You got any other symptoms? Cramps?"

Nan shook her head.

"What kind of curse?" asked Tim, sleepily.

That was too much! "How long have you been awake?" Nan demanded.

"I couldn't sleep with you yelling at Gramma," he mumbled. "Did you meet a witch or something while I wasn't around? What kind of curse is it?"

"The curse God put on Eve for picking the apple," said Gramma briskly. "Don't worry about it. It just means Nan's turning into a grown-up."

"Oh." Tim looked at her with interested, unfocused eyes. "Does that mean you're going to start wearing makeup and hogging the phone?"

"You shut up," snapped Nan. "This is private girl business."

"Don't get all huffy," said Gramma, opening the back door. "A couple of months from now you'll see it's not such a big deal. You won't be able to go swimming till it's over, but I don't see that anything else has to change."

76

"No swimming!" Nan followed her inside. "But Livvy and I were going to—I'll die if I can't go swimming!"

"It's only for a week. Just be glad it's me has charge of you and not your great-gramma. She always made us go to bed the first day of our time, just like we were sick."

Nan stumped upstairs and ran the shower, aquifer or no aquifer. If she'd mess up a swimming pool, she'd mess up a bathtub that much faster. She still ached, and she hadn't got near enough sleep, and why in heck couldn't Tim have just stayed asleep like he usually did? If Gramma wasn't too cheap to have air conditioners in the bedrooms, he wouldn't have known anything. She let the water run wastefully while she took inventory of her body. Her chest was swelling all right, and she was definitely getting hairier—why hadn't she paid any attention to that before? She would have to start wearing those stupid training bras Mom had made her pack. Well, anyway, she wasn't going to shave her legs or use makeup. Nobody could make her!

The morning got no better. Tim had tried to be helpful by fixing breakfast, but he had torn the soft figs to shreds while washing them and had made the toast too early and buttered it too late. The sanitary napkin Gramma brought her was uncomfortable. Nan spilled grape juice on her good dress, and the only other dress she had brought had gotten too tight across the shoulders in the last couple of months. Gramma made her hurry to catch the bus, and that made her mad, too. "Just once we could drive to church," she said, glaring at her sandals. She had meant to polish them that week but had never gotten to it. They looked awful.

"I never drive downtown if I can help it," said Gramma, testing the door to see that she had locked it. "Certainly not since they started tearing up the streets."

"There's no law says we have to go all the way downtown."

"I've been going to First Baptist all my life long," retorted Gramma, hurrying them down the sidewalk, "and I'm too old and cranky to change now. It won't hurt you to ride a bus. Big Daddy used to bus everywhere he could, to save money."

"Well, hurray for Big Daddy," muttered Nan.

The church had been built over the last hundred years or so, all in sprawling red brick, and in Nan's opinion barely looked like a church at all. They met Aunt Faith and Stella (not Bob—he was Catholic) in the patio. Nan yawned, responding to Aunt Faith's questions about Sea World without enthusiasm.

"I bet you don't feel like talking to any old grownups," said Aunt Faith, with a wise air. "Why don't you two run on to Sunday school, and we'll see you in church?"

"Nan's a grown-up herself, now," said Tim.

"Shut up!" Nan kicked him, without thinking, and harder than she'd meant to.

"You'd better straighten up, young lady!" warned Gramma.

"Sorry," Nan mumbled.

Tim followed her to the Sunday school building. "I liked you better when you were a kid."

"Stop saying things like that," Nan ordered. "It's not anybody's business, and it's not a big deal."

"You act like it is. Anyway, what is it? Gramma wouldn't tell me."

"That's because it's nothing boys need to know about." She glared over her shoulder, and saw Gramma, Aunt Faith, and Stella with their heads together, laughing. A rush of pure fury went through her. She was as sure as if she could hear them that they were discussing her morning's mistake. She would have let the door bang behind her if Tim hadn't caught it. Without returning the smiles of the people she passed, she headed straight for the door on the opposite side of the building.

Tim hurried to keep up with her. "Where are you going? Your Sunday school's that way."

"I'm not going to Sunday school," said Nan, feeling safe under the babble of voices.

"But—Gramma'll kill you!"

"Not if you don't tell her. I've got my watch on. I can be back in time for church." She pushed through the glass doors onto the street, not looking back to see how he took this.

People were coming in on this side, too. She needed to get away before some friend of Gramma's noticed her. With a long, purposeful stride, as if on legitimate business, she made her way through the crowded parking lot (few church members shared Gramma's determination not to drive downtown) to the river entrance and clattered down the stone steps.

It was the last entrance on this side of the River Walk, right across from the El Tropicano Hotel, and a long way from the stores and restaurants. Despite the drought, water rustled over a low weir and shrubs flowered sweetly, their fragrance mingling with the smell of bacon from the hotel. Nan took a deep breath. The San Antonio River was her idea of a creek—but whatever you called it, it was better than having to be polite in Sunday school! She set off briskly.

It was hard to believe a city could be so quiet; but street construction was halted for Sunday, most of the businesses were closed, and the tourists were only just beginning their day's idling. When she found a place to sit on the edge of the sidewalk and float her feet in the green, warm water, no one was around to stop her. When she came to the double cypress where (according to a tile mural) a Mexican sniper had picked off Texans as they tried to cross, no one was around to keep her from climbing into it, leaning along the trunk, and carefully firing her arm at invisible cowboys. She tried, unsuccessfully, to imagine what the spot would have been like before the tall buildings huddling over the river were built. When she and Tom figured out the rules of time travel she would come back and see for herself. A lone white duck swimming aimlessly in the middle of the river decided Nan ought to have food and came begging. Feeling guilty for misleading him, Nan went up to street level, still considering time travel.

She was sure Tim's poems were at fault, but since he wouldn't admit it, she was just going to have to figure out what was wrong with them, herself. She bought a Sno-Kone and trailed aimlessly through the streets, thinking.

You couldn't find two poems much more different than the ones about Grampa's pipe and Aunt Marian's heel. They both rhymed, but then so did the ones that didn't work, so that wasn't the important thing. Nan sucked on a piece of pineapple-flavored ice and rubbed the trunk of the painted elephant in front of Hertzberg's Circus Museum. They had known all about Grampa's pipe, but they hadn't known anything about the heel. Wait—no—they'd known a couple of things, like color, and they'd figured out other things that had turned out to be true, like its coming off at a party. Not one of Tim's bonfire poems had been true like that, or even as true as he could have made them. That might make a difference. It was worth a try.

Sweat tickled under the tight shoulders of her dress, and her heel hurt as if she were starting a blister. What had made Gramma so mad she'd wanted to wreck her own things? Nan couldn't guess—but she knew just how that mad had felt. She was lots better, now, but all she had to do was think of the laugh that had greeted her fear that morning. Burn! Smash! Scorch! Crash! She walked hard, in time to the rhythm.

She had finished her Sno-Kone and was examining the

displays in the ornate windows of Dillard's department store—her head trying to decide whether to ache, or to supply her with the next rhyme—when she was startled by a wafting of bells. That would be the Catholic church around the corner, the one Gramma mysteriously referred to as Saint Joske's. She glanced at her watch; and her head immediately opted to ache. The little gray screen that should have flashed the time at her was blank. The church bells kept ringing.

For a moment Nan turned, bewildered, in the middle of the sidewalk, jostling tourists. Going by river had upset her sense of direction, and she was no longer sure where she was. With an effort she got a grip on herself. She'd been here before. Dillard's was part of River Center Mall, where she and Livvy had come to spend her birthday money. They had come out of Dillard's and been able to stop and look at the Alamo dig a few yards away. She walked toward the gleaming cenotaph commemorating the Alamo heroes, and squinted at the skyline until she located the airy heights of the old Southwestern Bell building, which she passed on her way to church every week. All she had to do was head that way, and she'd soon get straightened out. Her heart quailed at the thought of Gramma's ire, and she began working out self-justifications as she hurried through the sun-struck streets.

Nan had never really explored downtown, and the on-going construction would have confused her anyway. A couple of the streets she crossed might have been in Cairo for all she knew of them. Then she saw the green square of Travis Park, and the Confederate soldier, pointing heavenward, soaring in the center. She squeaked with relief. The soldier had his back to Saint Mark's Episcopal, which was right across the street from Southwestern Bell. Then —she was too hot and out of breath to keep up her pace, but she clopped stubbornly along, panting—there was the Municipal Auditorium, and then her church. She hoped she wouldn't arrive in the middle of the service. Gramma would be furious—but at least she couldn't say anything in church. Serve her right if she worried, anyway. You couldn't make a Methodist go to Baptist Sunday school. It was in the Constitution.

The enormous flag by the Vietnam Memorial lay limp against its thick black pole. A cluster of tourists read the plaque. Nan had to pause, bending over a stitch in her side. Ick—she was going to be all nasty and sweaty in church. She cut across the short grass toward the auditorium—a funny-looking building, better suited to Iraq than to south Texas. Beyond its creamy walls she could see the red brick of the church, and a quick-pacing figure turning its head anxiously. Nan said a Spanish bad word that Livvy had taught her. Gramma had come looking for her!

The tourists took a picture and drifted across the plaza to the auditorium. Nan squared her shoulders and set her teeth, striding forward. Was it her fault San Antonio was hard to get around in? Could she help it her watch had stopped?

Gramma sighted her. "Where have you been? You get over here right this minute!"

The little girl trailing at the end of the group of tourists looked over her shoulder. Nan did not quicken her pace, but the anger started burning again. Gramma waited for her, arms akimbo and face like a thundercloud, on the broad walk leading to the auditorium entrance. Nan meant to meet her face-to-face, but Gramma looked as if she had never smiled. "I meant to be back in time for church," Nan said to the crisscross pattern of red, blue, and tawny tile beneath her feet. "My watch stopped."

"Just what's got into you, Nanna Elizabeth Bragg?"

"Nothing." She wished Gramma wouldn't talk so loud. She could hear one of the tourists reading from a plaque about some war dead the auditorium was in memory of, and if she could hear that, they could certainly hear Gramma scolding her. "I didn't want to go to Sunday school, that's all."

"Oh? I thought maybe you were trying to prove you were still a little kid, after all."

Nan did look up now. "I'm plenty old enough to decide if I want to go to Sunday school or not, so you just shut up and leave me alone!"

Gramma slapped her. The tourist girl was still looking at them, and the sound rang across the plaza. The sting

84

remained on Nan's cheek all through church, and all the way home, and all through dinner. She was perfectly calm, though, because she knew what she was going to do.

Sunday dinner didn't taste as good as usual, and drying dishes in silence while Gramma and Tim talked about cats took forever. As soon as she could she headed to the artifact collection, and took out number fifteen—the penny doll. In her neat, legible cursive, she wrote out her poem and made a couple of minor changes. On her way to the back porch, she remembered about her useless watch, and left it on the table. Tim was on the back steps brushing Satchmo.

"Come on," Nan said. "We're taking another time trip."

"How?" asked Tim. "We don't have any good artifacts."

"The artifacts are fine. It's your poems that are no good, and I'll prove it." Nan thrust her poem into his free hand. "That'll get us there all right."

Tim stopped brushing. Satchmo chewed the brush. Nan could tell from his face that Tim didn't like her verse at all, but she didn't care. "That won't work," he said. "That's ugly."

"Gramma was in an ugly mood and she did an ugly thing," Nan pointed out. "It's a true poem, and I bet anything that's what we need. Anyway, it's worth a try."

Tim shifted on his haunches. "I—I don't want to go back to then. I don't like it."

"How did I ever get saddled with such a wimpy

85

brother?" Nan demanded. "How did you ever even get to be part of this family? You don't want to go because you don't want to see the stuff burned. They're just cheap toys, and it happened fifty years ago anyway, and you can cover your eyes, can't you? We don't even have to talk to Gramma. We can go exploring instead. How are we ever going to get it down to a science if you wimp out on me?"

"I am not a wimp!" protested Tim, so emphatically Satchmo jumped. "And it won't work, anyway!"

"Then it won't hurt you to try."

Disgruntled, Satchmo jumped off the porch and loped across the yard. Nan sat down next to Tim, holding out the penny doll. "C'mon. Just say it over with me three times, and if nothing happens I'll leave you alone."

"Oh, all right," Tim grumbled. He dangled his feet off the porch and leaned his head against the rail, frowning at the piece of paper in his hand.

"Burn! Smash!
Scorch! Crash!
Stupid little baby toys,
Nothing but trash!
Teacups in the fire,
Grind the doll to dust,
Got to break something,
Or else I'll bust!"

86

Tim's voice sounded thin, but the words felt good in Nan's mouth as she chanted them, once, twice, three times. The ripple began, and Tim faltered, but she only chanted louder, watching the world splinter, darken, and cool; watching the kaleidoscopic fragments of yard resolve themselves into an autumn evening, where a girl struggled with matches before a heap of wood and trash on the bank of the creek.

10
Bonfire

The girl—Gramma—only had to turn her head to see them. A dog began to bark inside. Hurriedly Nan led Tim off the porch and around the corner. They scurried to the street, followed by unexpected animal noises— cackling, bleating, barking.

Even there, Nan felt exposed. The area was too open, almost completely lacking the trees and vined fences that she was used to. Though other houses were visible, their house was the only one on the cul-de-sac, its large lot studded with unfamiliar outbuildings and smelling of live-stock. Even the stars between the clouds seemed strange. Normally, city lights reflected off the sky so that it didn't get dark enough to show stars. Now, when Nan looked toward town, she saw winking neon where she should have seen tree silhouettes and a hazy glow. She felt a little breathless.

"This is weird," said Tim, "and it's dark, and we don't have a flashlight. How are we supposed to explore if we can't see?"

"Quit whining," said Nan. "Kids used to run around loose on Halloween night all the time, and they didn't have flashlights. Granddad told me about it."

Nan was still in her church dress, but Tim had changed back into shorts and a T-shirt, and, though the night was not cold, it was too cool for shorts. Tim hunched his shoulders. "I think we should go home. We can change clothes, and get a flashlight, and come back on one of the broken dishes."

"We might not be able to," Nan pointed out. "I'm not going straight back now we're here."

"What are you going to do, then?"

Nan took a deep, sweet breath. "I'm going to go help Gramma get in trouble."

Tim just stood and looked at her, his mouth blankly open. "Why would you want to do that?"

"Because I feel like it. I can do whatever I want here. There isn't anybody has the right to tell me what to do. Even Gramma's just another kid."

"Big Daddy's still a grown-up."

"Big Daddy's not around. Besides, he doesn't know we're related."

"Well, I think it's stupid."

"Don't be such a nerd. You're going to miss every chance you have in life."

"I don't mind missing chances to do stupid things," said Tim, with surprising firmness. "I'm going home."

"Spoilsport! Bet you can't."

"Bet I can. I want to go home! I want to go home! I want to go home!"

Nan barely had time to be afraid that he would drag her with him. She saw the ripple take him, like a reflection dispersing across a wave, so that she stood alone in the dark street.

Suddenly, the night was colder, the barking of the dog more menacing. Nan rubbed her bare arms, shivering. He had looked like a ghost, fading away—and now she was all alone. Well, who needed Tim, anyway? She would make all her time trips by herself from now on, not bother with that big baby. Resolutely, she circled the house, waiting beyond the chicken coop till the dog stopped barking, and entered the yard as if she were coming from Livvy's as-yet-unbuilt house.

Gramma crouched over the infant flames, blowing on them encouragingly. With her square face and round glasses, she looked a little bit like Nan herself. Her hair was cut closer to her head, though, and curled untidily— not Shirley Temple ringlets, but natural curls that stood up where they should've lain flat. Her plaid dress had puffed sleeves and was getting too small. Her flushed, dirty face frowned resolutely.

Nan stood outside the circle of light wondering what

to say. Suddenly the wind veered and blew smoke up her nose, down her throat, and under her contacts.

Nan went into a frenzy of stamping, coughing, and blinking. She should have brought her solutions with her! If she had to take a contact out now, she'd have to put it back in with spit, and the mere thought made her cringe. She pressed and rubbed around her lids, her nose and eyes running.

When her vision cleared, she saw the girl staring at her with surprise and concern. "Are you okay?"

"I'm fine." Nan blinked, sniffed, and coughed one more time, to be sure. She felt some explanation was due; and the full truth would not work if, as she suspected, contact lenses had not yet been invented. "I've got real sensitive eyes. The smoke hurts them something awful." She wiped at her wet cheekbone with a knuckle.

"You want my handkerchief?"

Nan accepted, scrubbing at her face and blowing her nose.

"I'm Naomi. Who're you? And what're you doing in my yard?"

Nan faced the challenge of her tone boldly. "I'm the Wicked Witch of the West. What's the fire for? Burning scarecrows?"

Naomi (it was impossible to think of her as Gramma) laughed shortly. "I wish I'd thought of being Witch of the West. It's just how I feel!"

"You can be Witch of the East," suggested Nan.

"I don't know. That'd make us sisters, and I'm about fed up with sisters. Come around this side. You'll get more smoke in your eyes over there."

"What's wrong with sisters?" asked Nan, obeying.

"They desert you in your hour of need, that's what!" Naomi blew on the fire and fed it sticks. "Everybody deserted me tonight. Except the dog. Dogs don't count."

Nan squatted, considering what she would have said if she hadn't known the story. The firelight showed her the pile of toys awaiting sacrifice—paper dolls, dishes, and other paraphernalia such as might be found at the back of any toy chest. "Are these your sister's things?"

"No. They're mine." The fire was about right for marshmallow toasting. Naomi squatted back and regarded it with satisfaction. "I'm going to settle this once and for all!"

"Settle what?"

"Whether I'm a woman or a kid. Mama told me I'd become a woman months ago, but she doesn't treat me like one. When it's my turn to do the dishes, or she needs somebody to baby-sit my little brother, then she says I'm old enough to pull my weight. When I want to play rubber guns or air wars, I'm too old to run around playing with boys. But if I want to go to a night movie alone, or try some lipstick on and see how it looks—all of a sudden, I'm little again!"

"You're old enough to be left home alone at night," Nan pointed out.

"So who wants to be home alone on Halloween?" demanded Naomi. "I was supposed to go to Coral Faber's party with Becky, and this morning Mama decided I was sick and couldn't go! I'm fine—but I'm too young to make up my own mind about whether I'm well or not!"

"That's not fair!" said Nan. "What's she think is wrong with you? You look okay to me."

Naomi looked around with exaggerated caution, and leaned closer. "Mama thinks everybody should stay in bed all day the first day of their lady's time," she whispered. "I think that's stupid."

"If it'd been me, I wouldn't've let her know," declared Nan. "It's none of her business."

"I tried." Naomi's low voice grew fierce. "But I bled on the sheets and Becky saw me put them in the wash and told on me. So she gets to go to the party, and my big brother's gone to a dance, and my little brother's at a kid party, and Mama and Daddy'd planned all week to go to the Mae West movie, so everybody's out having a good time but me. And you know what they said?" Nan could only shake her head. " 'You're big enough now you don't need us to stay home with you!' "

"That's awful!" exclaimed Nan. "That's as bad as getting slapped in public!"

"Is that what your folks did to you?"

"Uh-huh. So I ran off. I'll go back, but I'm so far away they'll never find me before I'm ready. What're you going to do?"

"First thing is to get rid of all my toys. If they can't have it both ways, I can't, either, so I'm making a clean sweep."

"You're going to burn everything?"

"Naw. I packed away the good stuff to keep for my kids—the dolls and like that. But this"—she picked up a plate adorned with a cartoon woman made entirely of curves and curls—"who needs it? By the time I have kids, nobody'll even remember Betty Boop!" She laughed recklessly as she tossed it into the fire. Nan remembered Gramma's unhappy face bending over the charred remnants of those dishes. She got a certain bitter satisfaction at the thought, but couldn't connect Gramma with Naomi at all.

"That won't work right," she said. "You'll have to smash them, or they'll just turn black."

"Okay," said Naomi, snatching up a flat cowboy figure—wood covered in painted paper. Holding him by the feet, she lit into the dishes, raising a satisfying frenzy of noise that culminated in a wild whoop as she hurled the cowboy to the flames. "Tom Mix! Who needs him?"

Inspired, Nan grabbed a handful of magazine cutouts stiffened with cardboard and tossed them in. The fire flared up. "Paper dolls! Who needs them?"

"Pinwheels! Who needs them?"

94

They circled the fire, chanting and dancing Indian style as they burned tin Cracker Jack prizes, battered Old Maid cards, the Orphan Annie mug, a homemade gun that shot rubber bands, cigar-box furniture, a barely recognizable homemade stuffed Mickey Mouse, a whole family of penny dolls (one of which Nan took care not to smash first), a paddleboat made from a sardine can—a mountain of toys that had been welcomed and played with went up in a frenzy of flame and smoke. Anything, whether spark or plaything, that popped out of the fire was mercilessly stamped on. Even when the paddleboat was reduced to twisted scrap metal and all else was invisible in the heart of the fire, they continued circling and chanting, the chant turning gradually into a spirited, off-key rendition of "Who's Afraid of the Big Bad Wolf?" Smoke blew all about them, but Nan found she could dance with her eyes half closed, lenses protected by a fringe of lash.

At last Naomi danced herself to a halt, puffing. "Whoof! Now I've got an appetite! Help me put this out and we'll go get some pie."

They doused the pyre with a bucket of water, waiting ready to hand, refilling it twice at a cranky pump of whose existence Nan had previously been unaware. When the fire was safely quenched, Naomi led the way indoors, where Nan passed inspection under the suspicious nose of a large collie-shepherd mix.

The house was like something out of a dream, familiar, but distorted. Walls that should have been robin's-egg blue, crowded with Grampa's photos, were white now, sparsely decorated by drawings in black and white or washed-out colors. The kitchen floor had changed from brown-patterned tile to green linoleum, and the walls were papered in a complex green and orange design, rather than trellised yellow roses. The table was the same, but the stove was different—and there wasn't any refrigerator at all! Instead, Naomi got cider and pumpkin pie out of a wooden cabinet, lined with metal and breathing damp coolness.

Nan hid her discomfort by getting down plates. The bright Fiestaware plates usually stored at the top of the cupboard with the wedding china took the place of the everyday dishes she was used to. She sat down to a generous helping of pie with a feeling of festival.

"Were you going to do anything particular tonight?" asked Naomi.

Nan tried to remember what Granddad had told her about Halloween when he was a boy in Iowa. It had stuck in her head, because the wildness he described with such relish had been so completely out of character for him. "Oh, just raise Cain generally," she said, borrowing one of his phrases. "I don't reckon there's any outhouses around here to turn over?"

Naomi laughed. "'Fraid not! There's lots of other stuff, though. We could get some soap, and some chalk, and—"

A couple of times, as they laid their plans, Nan caught Naomi stealing glances at her clothes. Probably they looked funny to her, even apart from being too small and summery. That was okay, though. It was probably the dress that made Gramma remember her as being from the Hooverville.

Naomi had a real witch costume, put together for the lost party; but they had to improvise Nan a mask out of a cardboard visor (used to protect the eyes during rubber gun battles, and belonging to the nine-year-old Great-Uncle Ben) dressed up with crepe paper, broom straw, and flowing cheesecloth. Naomi also tactfully loaned her a sweater and a helmetlike hat—"In case it gets any cooler." The outfit, viewed in an unfamiliar mirror, made her feel more in sync with her surroundings. In it, she barely recognized herself.

At last they embarked upon the unsuspecting night, laden with a burlap sack apiece. "Aren't you going to lock the door?" asked Nan, as they descended the porch. The dog glumly watched them through the living room window.

"What for?" asked Naomi. "There's no burglars around here."

Nan remembered other things Granddad had talked about. "There might be gangsters."

"Not here." Naomi hesitated. "'Course, you never know where Bonnie and Clyde'll turn up. My daddy says they won't do it if it don't give them a chance to kill somebody, though."

Nan had only the vaguest recognition of the names

97

Bonnie and Clyde, but she didn't want to look ignorant. "You don't really think they could be around here, do you?"

"As well be here as anywhere," said Naomi solemnly, leading the way onto the street and down to the creek. "And they'd as soon shoot you as look at you, you know. I bet if we ran up and chalked their backs, they'd turn around and shoot us dead!"

"I bet they wouldn't," said Nan, regarding the dark void of the creek. "Why are you going this way?"

"We put a plank over the water for a shortcut. It takes too long to go down to the bridge. C'mon. You're not scared, are you, Westwitch?"

"No more'n you are, Eastwitch," said Nan stoutly, and plunged into weeds as high as her knees.

11
Sisters under the Skin

*T*hat night was like nothing Nan had ever done before. The first time she followed Naomi in slashing a chalk mark down the backs of a pair of total strangers she felt uncomfortable, but when they turned out to be neighbors of Naomi's who laughed and joined in, screaming, "Halloween!" she relaxed and began to enjoy herself. They scrawled timeless slogans ("Beware!" "Boo!") on windshields with soap; rigged windows with instruments that would tap like ghostly fingers in the breeze; and draped the finest, proudest house they could find with festoons of toilet paper (Nan's suggestion—Naomi had never heard of "wrapping" houses, but thought it a swell idea). Oddly, none of this felt like misbehavior, and no one they ran across treated it as such. All Nan's bad feelings had burned up with the paper dolls, leaving her filled with tingling inspiration— no defiance, no anger, no meanness—even when the sheeted Mexican boys chased them, and they turned the tables by means of an ambush.

Not that there weren't bad moments. They stopped to stamp out a fire in an empty lot, and had a hard time convincing the policeman who happened along that they hadn't set it themselves. Their raid on Coral Faber's party almost went wrong, when Becky recognized Naomi's voice in the groans beneath the windows, and led a counterraid against them.

The worst moment of the evening came when a man lurched out of an alley at them, smelling like something dead, waving a bottle, and wearing only a shirt. Naomi's mouth fell open, and she seemed to freeze to the street. Nan grabbed her hand and jerked her to life. They pelted toward the lights of a major thoroughfare, pursued by the mumbling, groaning sound the man made.

At the dimly lighted door of a corner grocery, they stumbled to a halt. Nan looked back. "I don't see him anymore," she said, letting go of Naomi's hand. "Ick! That was a close one!"

Naomi rubbed her arms inside the long, loose sleeves of her witch's robe. Cars passed on the street, but the store windows were dark behind their blue eagle stickers. "It was just some old d-drunk. I b-bet somebody stole his pants while he was asleep and he hasn't even noticed yet."

"Maybe," said Nan, who had been told over and over again what to do if something like this ever happened to her. "Maybe not. We ought to call the police about him. Have you got any change?"

"We can't call the police," objected Naomi. "They'll ask questions. Anyway, I don't want to think about it."

"Oh, don't be such a baby," said Nan, scornfully. "We don't have to tell them anything but where we saw him. I'll call if you're too chicken."

"I'm not chicken! I just don't want to call."

"But what if he meets some little kids and—you know—does stuff to them? It'll be our fault."

"Oh—all right. I think I've got a dime here." She fished in her pocket, under her witch dress, producing a roll of Life Savers, a penknife, some string, cookie crumbs, lint, three pennies, two nickels, and a dime. "I wish phone calls weren't so expensive," she grumbled, dumping everything but the dime back in. "There goes half my allowance."

"Hey, at least you get an allowance," said Nan, trying to sound like a Hooverville girl, but wanting to giggle. What could you buy with twenty cents? Gramma had started giving her five dollars a week from Mom and Dad when she turned twelve.

Naomi refused Nan's offer to make the call, and it was just as well, because Nan would have done it all wrong. The phone was in a booth like those in old Superman cartoons, and it had no list of emergency numbers printed on the side. They crowded in—Nan stepping on something that crackled underfoot—and Naomi dropped in her dime and waited, not even attempting to dial. "Operator, I need to make a police report, please. A real one. Honest. There's a drunk walking around with no pants on."

Nan picked up the pack of cigarettes she had stepped on—forest green, with a red circle like a target. "Stupid litterbugs," she muttered, looking for a trash can.

"Hey, that's still got some smokes in it!" exclaimed Naomi. "That's—oh, yes. Uh—I'd like to make a report."

There was no wastebasket. Nan stood holding the cigarettes, wishing she'd let them lie. When Naomi hung up, she immediately started digging in her pockets and burlap bag. "Did I give you the matches? Or did I leave them?"

"I think you left them," lied Nan. "These are all squashed, anyway."

Naomi pulled one out and rolled it between her fingers, trying to restore its shape. "The tobacco's okay."

"You're not going to smoke them, are you?"

"Why not?"

"They're bad for you."

Naomi squeezed past her through the door. "You don't believe that garbage about them stunting your growth, do you?"

"I don't mean that. I mean cancer, and lung disease, and heart attacks, and things."

"Those don't have anything to do with smoking." Naomi looked up and down the street, and picked a direction.

"They do, too! You ask a doctor!"

"Our doctor smokes. So does the nurse. I don't know any grown-ups that don't smoke."

"My folks don't."

"They must be Hard-Shell Baptists or something, then." Naomi led the way up a cross street, where dogs barked, jack-o'-lanterns grinned, and bloodcurdling laughter rang from an invisible source. She strolled up a private sidewalk, sending a dog into a hoarse frenzy, removed the lid from a jack-o'-lantern on the porch, and stuck the cigarette inside. Nan waited, shifting nervously from foot to foot. A window banged just as Naomi withdrew the lighted cigarette. "You kids git a move on!" snapped a voice. "I've had about enough of this!"

"Just going!" Naomi scurried back to Nan, shielding the glowing end of the cigarette from the breeze. As they proceeded, she put the unlit end in her mouth, inhaled, and removed it, choking. "Ugh! It takes getting used to, of course."

"I don't see why you'd bother," said Nan, assailed by hope. Maybe if she was real convincing now, when she went home, Gramma wouldn't be a smoker. That chance made it worth sounding like a goody-goody. "All it's going to do is take money you could use for other things and smell up your house and turn your lungs black."

"Oh, you don't know anything about it." Naomi took another, more cautious puff. "My mama says you shouldn't judge anything till you've tried it." Her third puff did not choke her. "Really, you ought to try this. It's kind of sweet."

Nan snorted, ignoring a prickle of curiosity. "It doesn't smell sweet."

"Oh, well, if you're going to be narrow-minded."

"I am not narrow-minded!"

Naomi looked at her challengingly. "Prove it."

"All right, I will!" declared Nan recklessly. She put the cigarette into her mouth and breathed in.

It was about five times nastier even than she had expected—sweet, yes, but nauseating, with an overlay of bitterness—and she had not expected it to be actually hot. Choking and sputtering, she dropped the cigarette and stamped on it.

"Hey!" yelled Naomi.

"That's the grossest thing I ever tasted!" wheezed Nan.

"If you didn't want it you could have just given it back!"

"You couldn't have liked that! You just want to look big!"

"Don't you tell me what I want, you stupid witch!"

"Stupid yourself! Stupid, stubborn, stinky old witch!"

They stopped in the middle of the street, glaring at each other. The wind blew cold on the back of Nan's neck, and she found her anger already cooling into anxiety. She had no idea where she was, or how long she'd been gone.

If Naomi walked off and left her, how would she get home? Should she say that she hadn't meant to stamp out the cigarette, but had done it without thinking? It was true, but it sounded feeble.

She was saved by indignant feline yowls and an appalling clatter. Nan jumped. "What's that?"

"Somebody's torturing some poor cat," said Naomi, gathering her skirts and sprinting heroically toward the sound.

Three big boys struggled to tie a string laden with cans to the tail of an angry and agile cat, a sight to make the stoutest heart quail. However, a shower of stones from behind the fences on either side of the alley, assisted by the cat's own claws and the lucky intervention of a sleep-deprived householder who fired a shotgun blast into the air at the height of the racket, ensured that virtue triumphed. Nan and Naomi regrouped at the end of the alley, out of breath and mutually satisfied.

Nan yawned hugely as they trudged down the street, and Naomi caught it from her. "Geez, I'm tired! You got anything else you want to do?"

"Eat," said Nan, rubbing below her itching eyes. "Do you know where we are?"

"I can get us to my house."

"Are you going to be in bad trouble?"

"Probably. I don't care. It was—ho-rum!—worth it."

Nan had never walked so much in her life before, and found, to her surprise, that it was making her fingers heavy and stiff. Though she was too warm under her sweater, her bare toes were icy. The string on her visor mask chafed one ear; but she was glad she had it on when a tall car pulled up beside them, three blocks from the house, and Big Daddy leaned out the window. He didn't look exactly like the *Spirit of the Place* picture, but she knew him at once.

Naomi started guiltily. "Uh—hi, Daddy."

He jerked his head. "Get in. You, too, whoever you are."

Unthinkingly, Nan got into the backseat after Naomi, realizing that she should have refused only after the car started moving. She felt behind her for seat belts. There were none.

Naomi was the first to break silence. "I guess everybody else is home now, huh?" She sounded a little deflated.

"Yep," said Big Daddy.

"I didn't do anything wrong. You can whale me if you want, but I won't say I'm sorry."

"We can discuss all that at home."

Naomi subsided against the seat, chewing her lip. Nan remembered she was wearing things that didn't belong to her, and removed the hat, visor, and sweater.

"Did you—did you have to hunt for me long?" asked Naomi.

"I started around ten-thirty. It's past eleven now."

"Oh." Naomi slumped against the door. She didn't look like the Wicked Witch of the East anymore. But things could've been worse. Dad would've started bawling them out before they ever got into the car, and even Mom would've bombarded them with questions. Naomi was at least spared cross-examination before witnesses.

The house was fully lit when they pulled up. Big Daddy did not cut the motor. "Go on, Naomi. I'll take your friend home."

"No, thank you, sir," said Nan quickly, fumbling her first attempt to open the car door. She watched Naomi open hers, and succeeded in getting out the second time.

"Good night, Westwitch," said Naomi. "I'm glad you came along."

"Good night, Eastwitch," said Nan, sincerely. "I'm glad I came, too."

Big Daddy had gotten out of the car, but he still hadn't turned the engine off. As the front door closed behind Naomi, he said: "You'd better let me drive you home, sister. Where do you live?"

Nan swallowed. He was not a tall man—not much taller than her—but she knew what Gramma had meant when she said he was the boss man. It was in the way he spoke, and stood, and looked right at her from under brows as straight as rulers.

"I'm sorry, sir. I can't tell you that."

"Are you lost?"

"No, sir. I can get home all right."

He looked at her and she felt that each eye was a drill, driving into her brain through her own eyes. It was all she could do to meet his gaze, much less say anything. "What's your name, sister?" he asked, with a surprising gentleness.

"Nanna Bragg, sir."

He sat down on the running board and patted the place next to him. Nan sat beside him, their clothes touching. He gazed out across the creek to the flashing downtown neon. "Halloween's not a good night for a girl to be out on her own, Nanna."

"I don't have to go far."

"You don't live around here. Why don't you let me take you home?"

"Because I really truly can't." Nan wondered if he would believe the whole truth; and, if not, what sort of lie would satisfy him. She found she did not want to lie to him one bit.

"You know, the whole world's got hard times. Lots of decent, hard-working people are living in shacks not good enough for a dog. As long as you do the best you can, there's no need to be ashamed, these days."

Nan realized that there was only one way to keep him from taking her home. She stood up. "I'm not ashamed of anything. I just can't let you. Thank you, anyway." She dashed into the dark, diving into the tall, dry growth along the edge of the creek, slipping and tumbling.

"Home! Home! Home!" she said to herself, as the long grass whipped past her ears and stones rattled her bones. Her body whirled and rippled, and when she rolled to a stop on the verge of the grubby water, the sky was early-evening-colored, and the air was heavy and hot.

Nan was tired, and being sent to her room with only bread and butter for supper was a perfectly reasonable punishment. She had been gone for over five hours, and she offered no plausible explanation. She couldn't blame Gramma for being mad.

Nan should have been asleep when Gramma came in later—it was past ten, and she certainly was tired enough. She was lying with her eyes closed, the scenes of her strange, dark day flickering through her head like an old movie, when she heard the boards creak outside her door. The hall light was off, but a dim strip, the last of the light from downstairs, entered the room. Gramma tiptoed in, laying something on the nightstand.

"Wha'smatter?" mumbled Nan.

"Shh. Go back to sleep. I didn't mean to wake you."

"S'all right. I wasn't." Nan yawned. "I'm sorry about today, Gramma."

"Yes. Well. I'm sorry I laughed at you this morning."

"You are?" Nan woke a little more.

"I wasn't thinking. I had a big sister to learn about these things from, and you don't. Anyway, I brought you something I got the year I became a woman. I thought you might like it."

Nan sat up. "What is it?"

"My copy of *Jane Eyre*. Did you ever read it?"

"Not yet." Nan picked it up. It was too dark to see the book, except as a black shape, but it felt smooth and sturdy in her hands and smelled good.

"You'll like it. It's one of the three best books in the world."

Nan smothered another yawn, trying to force an intelligent remark through the wool in her brain. "What're the other two?"

"*Little Women* and the Gospel of John. Good night, snickerdoodle."

"Good night, Gramma," said Nan into the warm solidity of her hug.

12
The Mysterious Elk Clip

Satchmo sprawled on his back, legs flopping open like the covers of a book. Nan sat beside him on the back steps, her notebook in her lap, her hair sticky on her forehead and neck. Livvy had gone home for the evening. The air smelled of baked chicken. Weighed down by heat and a sense of futility, she read over what she had learned about time travel. It didn't look like much.

I. An artifact can only be used once.
II. An artifact must be associated with some event.
III. An artifact must have been buried for an unknown period of time. Artifacts that have never been buried don't work; neither do those that have been buried on purpose, then dug up again.
IV. Tim and I must go together, but can return separately.

V. Poems don't need to be good, but must be true.

VI. Poems can be used twice.

VII. Objects from the past can be carried to the future.

They'd used her "Burn! Smash!" poem and a saucer to go back to that memorable Halloween again, just for a minute. It hadn't worked when they recited it in the street, but they'd gone into the house and from the room Gramma's brothers had shared, they'd looked out the window, and seen two wild figures dancing around a fire chanting, "Betty Boop! Who needs her?" They had taken with them a sock out of Uncle Jake's dresser—socks are always disappearing—and come back with it.

Nan had gotten energetic one day and written down a bunch of hypotheses on the page across from the rules, but they hadn't gotten anywhere toward proving them yet. It would take so long to test them all, and the weather was so hot!

Gramma rapped on the kitchen windowsill. "Dinner!"

Nan dragged herself in. "It's almost too hot to eat."

"It looks like it might rain," said Tim, sticking a postcard (showing camels and mountains) into his current book.

"It's looked like it might rain every evening for two weeks," grumbled Nan.

They joined hands, said grace, and passed the chicken. "Nights like this, we used to make rainmakers," said Gramma.

"What's a rainmaker?" asked Tim.

"Don't kids play with those anymore? It's this piece of wood you whirl around your head on a string, and it makes a sound like thunder. Indians used them, I think, and—oh, whatdayacallems—those people in Australia. Aborigines."

"Did they make it rain?" It wasn't any weirder than time travel.

Gramma shrugged. "They don't hurt."

After the dishes were done, she showed them how to make a rainmaker. It didn't look like much, but thundered satisfactorily, and the wind actually rose as they whirled it. Nan smelled rain, but it wasn't the first time that month. Tomorrow would be just like all the days preceding it.

Only it wasn't.

During the night half-hearted drizzles made them get up and shift their cots, but did not make them retreat inside. The morning was somewhat cooler. Gramma was showing Nan how to make a farmer's breakfast when the hiss, rattle, and roar of a real downpour began. Tim ran in from the porch waving his book and laughing. "It's raining! It's pouring! The old man is snoring!"

Nan wanted to run out and dance. Satchmo—usually the sedatest of cats—dashed up and down stairs as if his tail were afire. Tim kept jumping up to look out the window and actually ate as much breakfast as Gramma thought he should. Gramma's hair went from limp to fluffy in five minutes, and her face changed from the flushed red of the past month to a bright, lively pink. While Nan and Tim did breakfast dishes, she opened the ancient hi-fi record player in the living room and put on a stack of old-fashioned, thin-sounding records—Louis Armstrong, Benny Goodman, Glen Miller, and some oddities, such as "Over the Rainbow" played by a swing band. When Livvy came over, fleeing the shut-in racket of her brothers, Gramma taught them all to jitterbug.

In the afternoon the sun came out, glittering over the wet world. Gramma chased everyone outside. "This house is filthy!" she said. "Don't know how I ever let it get so bad. Scat now! I've got work to do."

"Let's dig for more doll dishes," suggested Livvy. "The ground's nice and soft now."

"I think we got everything that survived the fire," said Nan, "but there's plenty of squares left. We might find something just as good."

She dug what was left of 4N6E, which had held part of the bonfire, while Livvy and Tim started fresh in 2N6E and 2N5E. The book said each square should be dug as a square hole, with straight sides and sharp, ninety-degree angles at each corner. It wasn't easy, but Nan worked hard, and kept reminding the others to be careful. Tim and Livvy were more interested in finding something than they were in doing the job right. Nan found more charcoal, and a piece of metal that might have been broken off a

114

garden claw. Livvy found some rocks that might be unfinished arrowheads, and Tim got the prize of the day—a tie clip, rusted all into one piece, and the paint on the round part half gone. They made out a purple border, a star, a stag's head superimposed on what might be a clock face, and some letters, on the identity of which they couldn't agree—either RFOE, BRQE, or RPOF.

Livvy had gone home—taking half the potential arrowheads as her choice of payment for her labor—and Nan was finishing up her record-keeping when Gramma came out to shake her duster and plump down into a lawn chair. "Whoof! I'm tired! But at least the house is clean." She didn't look near as worn out as she had during most of July. "What say we all get cleaned up and go out for dinner? I know where they make the best onion rings in town."

"Can we shower?" asked Nan, looking down at the havoc digging had wreaked upon her.

"Mmm. I don't know. Look how dry the ground is already—just sucked all that rain up and wants more. Did y'all find anything interesting?"

Tim, in charge of labeling and wrapping specimens, showed her the results, saving the tie clip for last. "And I found this!" he said proudly, putting it into her hand. "What does BRQE stand for?"

"Oh my goodness," said Gramma softly, taking it in her palm. "The things y'all turn up! This is Big Daddy's

115

old Elk Lodge clip. It must be his—your grampa never would join. That's BPOE on the bottom there—Benevolent and Protective Order of the Elks."

"What's it doing out here?" asked Nan. "Did he lose it?"

"No. No, my mama threw it away." Gramma rubbed the clip with a corner of her apron. "It must've fallen out of the trash and got trampled in the garden. Your great-gramma kept a garden through the depression right up to the end of the war."

"What business did she have throwing it away?" demanded Tim. He was a great hoarder himself, and Mom didn't dare throw out so much as a pair of ragged slippers without checking first.

"None, I don't reckon, but she was mad—my land, was she mad! Big Daddy was so surprised when she started yelling it took him fifteen minutes to yell back, and then didn't they go at it! Us kids were supposed to be in bed —we were all mostly grown by then, but he'd come home late. We gathered in the boys' room and listened with our mouths open. First time either of them'd ever raised a voice at the other—last time, too, thank goodness!"

"What were they fighting about?" asked Nan.

"Politics," said Gramma, shutting her mouth tight. She handed the clip back to Tim and said, in an ordinary voice, "Why don't y'all go clean up? One of you can use the tub upstairs and the other one can use the downstairs."

Nan's curiosity was piqued, but Gramma would not

give in to it. The rebuffs her well-planned, innocent-sounding questions met at dinner and before bed convinced her that, whatever Big Daddy and Great-Gramma had fought about, it was nothing as boring and ordinary as politics. She had a way of finding out, of course—but there was no hurry. This time she and Tim would do it right.

"What d'you mean, do it right?" asked Tim, when she sat on the edge of his bed after he was supposed to be asleep.

"Last couple of times we haven't dressed right," Nan explained. "We had to make up stories off the tops of our heads when people noticed us. We got lucky, but what if we hadn't?"

"So what?"

"So we don't know what. Maybe we could change history. Maybe we go back to the middle of World War II and some general sees us and finds out about time travel and the world as we know it changes. We don't know so we can't chance it. So what we've got to do is, we've got to get costumes, and we've got to make up cover stories, so we'll fit in."

"I don't see how. We don't even know when this happened."

"We know generally. Gramma said Great-Gramma must've dropped it in the garden; that means it's before the end of the war and she said all the kids were mostly grown up, so it can't be very long before the war, either."

"Where are we going to get costumes? You can't sew."

"You let me worry about that. Your job is to make up cover stories and a poem. A true poem, remember—don't go sticking in stuff that wasn't there."

"How do I know what was there? I don't even know what the fight was about!" grumbled Tim. But she could tell by the way he looked past her at nothing that he had set his mind to his part of the problem.

It wasn't hard to get Gramma to drag out the old photo albums and take her on a tour of the family pictures. There were fewer of these for the years of and before the war than for later times, because Grampa wasn't around; but Gramma's inability to throw anything out stood her in good stead. Once the pictures were being looked at, it was the most natural thing in the world to ask about clothes and hair. Gramma not only told her about the proper length of dresses and the place of jeans in the scheme of things, but showed her how to make spit curls.

Nan had hoped for boxes of old clothes in the attic but, although it was much cooler (only in the mid-nineties) it was still too hot to go up and look for them, and even if it hadn't been, Gramma didn't think they would find anything. "Use it up, wear it out, make it do, or do without!" chanted Gramma. "If we outgrew it before it fell apart, there were plenty of people to hand it down to, believe me. I've got the mitt from Mama's wedding dress, but that's the only stitch I ever kept. There's too many naked kids in this world for that."

But Nan had no problem getting permission to use the beaded purse and old barrettes that she found down at the back of the cedar chest. A little experimentation persuaded Nan that she could make Tim and herself look acceptable, if not exactly fashionable, with these accessories and the right combination of modern clothes. Tim fussed over the poem a lot, studying the dictionary and the poetry books in the living room, and in two days had something he and Nan agreed would probably work. They decided to try during Gramma's weekly floor mopping. There was no telling how long they needed to be gone, and Gramma should be willing to grant them permission to stay out for quite a while that day.

Sure enough, Gramma was only too glad to get them out from underfoot, and never questioned their sudden desire to go to the wax museum downtown, or the way they chose to dress for the occasion. She turned them loose with their full allowances and a little extra in Nan's bead purse, and the usual warnings about strangers. She didn't even wait to see in which direction they went.

No one was in the channel of the creek just now. They helped each other down the slope, and adjusted their costumes. Nan had spent some of her allowance on ankle socks and had put on her best shoes. The second-best dress was called into service again, this time with a belt added and the lace collar removed. Tim had to wear a button shirt, with his jeans, and his old sneakers that tied, rather than his new, Velcro-fastened ones. "We don't look like we belong together," he complained. "You're too dressed up."

"Girls did dress up more in those days. Come on."

They held hands, although they knew it wasn't necessary, stood shoulder to shoulder, glanced around to be sure they were unobserved, and chanted:

"We found the Elk clip where Great-Gramma
       dropped it,
   five inches down, below the garden soil,
   and wondered why Big Daddy didn't stop it,
   but let her throw it out during the roil
   of their lost tempers. We wonder why they
       fought,
   what Big Daddy could've done to make her
       shout.
   She always did exactly what she ought—
   until the day she threw that tie clip out."

Nan's heels began to ripple.

13
Following in Their Footsteps

*T*he air was evening-warm rather than afternoon-hot. The pecan under Nan's room was no higher than the window of the sewing room below. Otherwise, the world appeared much the same. Nan dropped Tim's hand and twisted her spit curls one more time. "Ready?"

"Uh—I guess."

If he had asked her that, she would have replied: "For anything!" For a poet, Tim was not much good at dramatic dialogue. They helped each other up the slope, but stopped to survey the land before actually reaching the top.

They were just in time to see Big Daddy come onto the porch. They knew he was Big Daddy at once, even at a distance. "No telling," he said, over his shoulder. "Don't wait up for me."

"I just hope you don't regret it," said the woman behind him. Great-Gramma was pretty, but tired-looking, her hair smooth on top with big curls on her shoulders. A tall young man came out after her and waved to Big Daddy as he headed up the street.

"She doesn't sound mad," said Tim softly.

"She won't be till he gets home," Nan reminded him. "Let's let him get as far as the corner before we follow him."

"What if he takes the car?"

There was a blue car in the driveway, less big than the one that had picked Nan up on Halloween, but still massive. Big Daddy walked right past it. As they lay low among the tall weeds, the boy turned on the hose to water the grass; and a teenage girl in a swirly skirt came out the back door to take clothes off the line. Nan's arms prickled. "That's Gramma," she said, nudging Tim, "and I bet that's Great-Uncle Jake that died on Guam."

Tim regarded the future war fatality with interest. "He looks like one of Mom and Dad's students, except for the dorky haircut."

"It's probably a real cool haircut, whenever we are. Come on. Try to look like you belong here."

They brushed off their clothes and walked out onto the street. Their house was no longer the only one on the cul-de-sac, but the others looked brand new. The air smelled of sawdust, most of the yards were beds of dirt, and some of the windows were still marked with chalk. Jake smiled at them as Big Daddy disappeared around the corner. "Evening."

Nan ducked her head back at him. "Evening." She had a sudden fear that they would be stopped—that they would lose Big Daddy and be alone in this slightly skewed reality. "C'mon," she said to Tim, trying to sound carefree, "race you to the corner!"

Nan won, coming to a panting halt on the big white letters of the word STOP on the pavement. Big Daddy stood at a bus stop marked with a round sign halfway down the block. The approaching bus looked like it should belong to the army, not the city, but it was slowing down for him. They barely had time to run up and climb on after Big Daddy.

Nan started to pull change out of her beaded purse, and was struck by a terrible thought. She had enough money to get into the wax museum and buy some ice cream, about twelve dollars, but not a bit of her money had been made yet! She stopped with her fingers in the depths of the purse as the doors closed behind them and the bus lurched forward. Maybe no one would notice the dates—but what if they did? Anyway, it would be dishonest.

"C'mon, sis," said the driver helpfully. "Nickel apiece. Or have you got tickets?"

"N-no," said Nan, thinking furiously. "I lost them."

Tim squeaked. "You dummy! How could you lose so much money?"

"I didn't mean to! I've got—I've got a hole in my purse."

"Can't let you ride without a fare, honey," said the driver. "Sorry."

"But we've got to get downtown," said Tim, primed with a cover story. "We're supposed to meet our mom in front of the Alamo, and we're late already."

"Here." Big Daddy fished in his pocket and put two nickels in the box.

Nan looked up at him gratefully. "Thank you, sir."

"'S all right. Can't have your mama worrying about you, can we?" Nan was surprised to see that he had blue eyes. She had always assumed they were brown, like hers. His face just then did not look like hers at all. It was too serious, and kind, and grown up. "Y'all be sure to stick to Alamo Plaza, now. Whatever you do, don't go near Auditorium Circle tonight."

Nan and Tim sat down a couple of seats behind Big Daddy, Nan at least tingling with pleased curiosity. What was going to happen at Auditorium Circle, that he warned total strangers away from, and Great-Gramma hoped he wouldn't regret? She wiggled on the slick, hard seat. She and Tim were the only kids aboard. There were several Mexicans, one or two black people at the very back, and four or five white people in the front. Only Big Daddy was fresh and vigorous looking, in clean white shirt-sleeves, the Elk Lodge clip on a plain black tie, and a white hat.

"You really think there'll be trouble?" asked the bus driver.

"It can't be avoided now. The radio says the police have had to redirect traffic since five. The plaza's packed."

"Maybe Emma'll finally come to her senses and call it off."

Big Daddy snorted. "She can't back down now any more than we can."

A woman in a hat with a soaring brim said: "Seems to me this thing with Hitler and Stalin gives her a good reason. There's no way these Communists can claim not to be subversive now."

"Those Reds can claim anything," said Big Daddy, firmly.

The bus stopped and let on a teenage boy, his short, dark hair slicked back and glistening as if new washed. He had a camera around his neck. "Evening, Mr. Chadwell," he said, sitting down opposite Big Daddy.

"Evening, Persh. Where you off to this evening?"

"Same place you are, I reckon." There was something familiar about his voice.

Big Daddy shook his head. "That's no place for a boy."

"Neither were the trenches," said Persh. The woman in the hat flashed an approving smile at him. "I just want to see what's going on. I can take care of myself."

"It makes me sick that Mayor Maverick let things go this far," said the woman. "Why, I voted for the man! He was in the service himself. He ought to understand."

"He thinks he's doing right," said Big Daddy. "You can't blame a man for that."

"Then what are you off downtown for?" asked the bus driver.

"Just 'cause I can't blame him, that's no call for me to let him," said Big Daddy.

The conversation continued over their heads, all about brave men who died for their country and some disgraceful situation that Big Daddy was on his way to prevent. Nan couldn't understand what Great-Gramma was going to get so mad about. Dad often said that the world would be a better place if people would take action when they saw something horrible going on. Apparently somebody was going to do something horrible today, and Big Daddy was taking action. Maybe it had something to do with the war. She couldn't tell whether the war had started yet or not, but they certainly were concerned about defending the Constitution and the American government. The heat, and the smell of exhaust, and the effort of trying to sort out the conversation, made her head ache, and she kept her face turned toward the open window.

The streets had the same distorted, dreamlike quality as the house had on her last visit. Houses she knew as rundown now, or converted into businesses, sparkled with white paint, and had children playing in the yards; lots that should have held houses were empty; and long stretches of streets she knew she had been on were unrecognizable. Most of the streets had no stop signs, just STOP written on the pavement, and those she did see were yellow and black instead of red and white. There were quite a lot of flowers, but no trees, and the cars had pitifully small windows. It took her a while to figure out what was bothering her about the billboards and the people—after all, you expected the clothes and ads to be different—and they were almost downtown before it hit her. None of the billboards was in Spanish; and almost all the people she saw were white.

The traffic thickened, until they reached a corner Nan felt she ought to recognize, where a policeman directed the bus around a traffic jam. "All off for the rally," said the driver.

Big Daddy, Persh, and a couple of other people stood up. Nan considered whether they ought to get off, too; but they'd said they were going to Alamo Plaza. Persh bade the driver good night in an absent voice, checking the light meter on his camera; and suddenly Nan knew who he was. She leaned over and hissed in Tim's ear, "That was Grampa!"

Tim looked at her in surprise. "Hadn't you noticed that?" he asked. "He sounded just the same."

And of course Grampa's first name had been Pershing. Nan felt disgusted with herself. She would have to pay better attention. The bus crawled through congested, half-familiar streets, and let them off at its nearest approach to the Alamo.

Nan was surprised at how changed the plaza was. The huge white marble cenotaph was only half built; and it was astonishing what a difference the absence of River

Center Mall made. Dillard's was still there, with all its fancy windows—but it wasn't Dillard's. It was Joske's of Texas, bearing on its roof a huge, animated neon sign on which a cowboy roped a calf repeatedly.

"I hope you know where we're going," said Tim.

"All we've got to do is go toward the crowd," said Nan.

Their first choice of direction was blocked by a policeman who shared Big Daddy's opinion on children going to the rally, so they headed down Houston Street, walking close under the buildings to avoid being jostled by distracted grown-ups. That was how Nan came face to face with Judy Garland, on a poster announcing *The Wizard of Oz*—Coming Soon! They stood and goggled at it a minute. "You know," said Tim, in an awed voice, "I bet we're the only people in town who've seen that movie!"

Somehow this was the weirdest idea of all. Nan didn't even want to think about it. "We've come too far," she said. "We need to go that way."

Travis Park itself looked much the same, as far as they could tell for the crowds; but there was a bus station next to Saint Mark's Church, and the trees were shorter and fewer. As for the Southwestern Bell building beyond—it simply didn't exist. In its place was something shorter and less fancy that Nan couldn't get a good look at, because of the people in Auditorium Circle.

They packed the plaza, a surging, roaring mass trampling places that would be Vietnam Memorial and flower beds and a street. They were men and women and even a

128

few more children; lots of teenage boys; lots of men bearing lots of different insignia; white people and Mexicans; and a thin dark line of policemen, linking arms across the Auditorium steps. Nan, craning between tall grown-ups, only glimpsed them before a broad back in a business suit cut off what view she had.

"I don't believe this," said Tim. "How are we going to find them in this mess?"

Nan shook her head, any ideas she had overwhelmed.

14
The Fall of the Auditorium

*A*ll they could see were streaks of floodlights across the darkening sky. Nan grabbed Tim's hand and pushed and wiggled her way toward the rock wall behind Saint Mark's. ". . . came all the way from Atlanta for this," she heard one woman say, in passing.

". . . won't get away . . ."

"See, there was this traveling salesman . . ."

"Hey, got any more for a friend?"

Nan boosted Tim onto the wall. He stretched out flat and helped her up after him. They settled side by side above a woman holding a baby and a man holding a beer bottle. The plaza was a sea of heads—mostly bare, many in white hats or military-looking caps. Activity seemed concentrated around the end of the building nearest the Baptist church. Nan strained her eyes, trying to find Big Daddy and Persh.

Dusk gathered rapidly beyond the floodlights. Tim wiggled uncomfortably. "I hope it starts soon."

Nan bumped her shoes against the stone, trying not to kick the people below her. "You reckon this is something to do with the war?"

Tim made an elaborate, I-don't-know shrug.

Small in the distance, a man came out of the Auditorium onto the front steps in front of the police line, his light-colored suit standing out against their dark blue. Ignoring a couple of men who popped out of the crowd to take his picture, he talked into his hand, and a voice rang through the air, loud and distorted, like the school intercom.

"You people can see much better from the other side of the street. There's no more seats inside. I'm sure no one will cause trouble. Please move back."

A surge of noise went up. "Let us all in, we'll fill up the Auditorium!"

"Go back to Illinois!"

"Wheresh Emma?" called the man with the beer bottle below Nan and Tim.

"Who cares?" The woman shifted the baby. "Where's Mayor Maverick?"

A man struggled out of the crowd onto the steps and said something to the man in the light suit. Tim squinted. "That's a priest. Priests are always on the good side, aren't they?"

"I hope so," said Nan. The policemen opened a way for him to go in the side door. Other policemen chased off people scrambling on top of a white stone block to look in the window on that side. "The flower beds are getting trampled something awful," said Tim. "They're being awfully rude."

The woman with the baby turned unexpectedly. "Not near as rude as what's going on in there," she said, in a loud, strained, eager voice.

"What is going on in there, ma'am?" asked Nan.

"Spitting on gravestones," said the woman. "My daddy's gravestone!" The baby began to cry.

A hatless, pudgy man in short sleeves edged his way to the front, shook off a policeman, and waved his arms, his mouth moving inaudibly. The miscellaneous roar of the crowd steadied out as a song spread over the plaza. The tune was "I Been Working on the Railroad," but the words, when Nan finally sorted them out, were not the same.

> "The eyes of Texas are upon you,
> Till Gabriel blows his horn!"

The crowd cheered and clapped—even the woman with the baby patted his back in an applauding rhythm—and the man with the beer bottle whooped and drank. The man in shirtsleeves began waving his arms again.

> "My country, 'tis of thee,
> Sweet land of liberty,
> Of thee I sing!"

Nan and Tim began to sing along. The plaza became quiet underneath the shared music. Nan's heart swelled to include everyone around her. Whatever was going on here, she was part of it, part of these united, purposeful people.

They sang "The Star-Spangled Banner" next. The darkness was complete. At the side of the building the song trailed off, grew ragged, melted into shouts, catcalls, boos. Nan stopped singing and strained her eyes, but she couldn't see what was happening—just people milling around, and a blink of bright light like a camera flash. A cheer rose—from inside the building?—and was drowned by cries from outside. Only a few voices finished the national anthem. The pudgy song leader had disappeared.

"Lynch 'em! Kill the Reds!"

"Let's go! Let's go!"

A man—a short man—scrambled atop the white stone under the window. His voice rang clear and authoritative over the crowd. "Let's wait till she opens her damn mouth and if we don't like it, then rush her!"

Nan leaned forward. "Big Daddy?" she breathed.

Someone waved a military-looking hat. Other hands waved other things—sticks, rocks, fists—and all words vanished in a throatless, sourceless howl. Tim pointed at the roof. "Why are there firemen up there?"

"Maybe they're afraid somebody'll set the building on fire."

Through the roar floated the sound of singing—small

133

and muffled. "Good, they're singing 'The Star-Spangled Banner' again," said Tim.

Nan sat up straight. "No, they're not. Those're the people inside the building."

Big Daddy—if it was he—jumped down. Beyond him, the windows shattered, the crash of breaking glass drowning out the "rockets' red glare." The woman with the baby cheered. The man with the beer bottle pushed into the crowd as it surged forward. A wave of people rushed the side of the building, sending bricks and stones ahead of them. Between the floodlight beams a fireman shouted something over his shoulder. A blast of water burst from the roof and another from the windows. Bricks and stones still flying through the air, the mob retreated a few yards.

Someone—a silhouette among the floodlights—rose above the crowd near the door, the shape of his head distorted by a lifted camera. Despite the rocks flying like moths all around him, he fiddled with the big, clumsy box swiftly and calmly, like Grampa on a Christmas morning. Just as his flashbulb went off, something jerked his head forward. He staggered, and fell into the seething mob.

Nan almost screamed, closing her mouth on it just in time. Tim cried out. "Grampa! Was that Grampa?"

"Of course not!" snapped Nan. "His camera was lots littler!" But how did she know? She'd barely seen him— he was so far away, and the light so distorting—she bit into her lip till the pain made her stop.

134

Tim wiggled forward on the wall. "You can't be sure! I'm going to go help him!"

Nan seized his arm in both hands. "No, you aren't! You want to get trampled to death?"

"But—if it's Grampa—"

She shook him, realizing the truth barely in time to speak it. "We know he'll be all right! We know what happens to him! But we don't know what happens to us! So we're not taking any chances! We're going to sit tight, you understand me?

Tim looked out over the plaza, where rocks and giant streams of water dodged in and out of the light, and set his jaw. Nan tightened her grip, sick to her stomach. She shouldn't have brought him here. If she'd known—but how could she have guessed Big Daddy would be involved in a riot?

She felt the muscles in Tim's skinny arm bunching to tear loose. Suddenly through the racket of the crowd, the hoses, and the breaking glass came the squeal of tires and the roar of an engine. An open car tore around the building, the crowd scattering before it. Blasts of water drenched the people inside the car, but it did not slow down.

A policeman ran toward the car, waving his arms and blowing a whistle shrilly. The car skidded, so close that the puddles under the tires spurted over him, and he had to jump back. The mob howled. "Run over him! Kill him!" Tim's arm ceased to resist, as the car roared off again, the teenage boy in the passenger seat waving wildly at the cheering throng. The space they had cleared closed after them. Part of the crowd started chanting, "We want Maverick!"

Nan looked at Tim. His eyes were closed. "It's all right," she said. "They didn't run over anybody. This time."

He opened his eyes. "But what were they doing? Why would anybody want to kill a policeman?"

"How do I know?" snapped Nan.

"These people can't be on Big Daddy and Grampa's side," declared Tim, plaintively. "They can't. Grampa wouldn't ever hurt anybody!"

A new development kept Nan from having to answer. A ripple of movement along the line of policemen preceded clouds of fine smoke rising from the pavement. "Get out your handkerchief, dear," said a grown-up voice nearby. "I think they've started chemical warfare."

"Oh, how thrilling!"

Startled by the tone of these voices, Nan turned her head. A man in a tuxedo and a woman in a long dress were watching the commotion with rapt faces. The man took a large handkerchief out of his pocket, and the woman a small one out of her uselessly tiny purse. "This is lots more interesting than that party was! Do you really think any of the gas will get all the way over here?"

"Depends on how the wind blows," said the man solemnly, through his handkerchief.

"Sickos," hissed Nan. Sections of the crowd were coughing now, staggering, but still pressing forward, toward the Auditorium and the frail, nearly invisible shadows of the police. "Cover your face up, Tim. I think they're using tear gas."

"I hope it works," said Tim, unbuttoning his shirt and draping it over his head.

Nan had no handkerchief, and could hardly hike her skirt up to her face. In the glimpses she dared to take between her nearly shut lashes, she saw people staggering, crying, rolling up their pant legs to splash through puddles, cheering, throwing rocks, standing still and watching—but no one leaving. The PA system rumbled and squeaked futilely into the night, as two men barely visible behind a protective wall of policemen took turns pleading with the crowd to go home because the meeting was over.

At last the defenders gave up. The PA system fell silent, the policemen vanished inside, and the sounds of breaking glass and shouting ruled supreme. People hurled themselves against the solid wood doors, pounding with fists and shoulders. The firemen retreated from the edges of the roof, and the streams of water ceased. A mist hung over everything, swirling in the light, warm breeze. Nan bent over to wipe her stinging eyes with her skirt.

After a long time the priest appeared on the balcony— she thought it was the same priest. He waved his arms and ducked down behind the rail to avoid a shower of stones. After several repetitions his voice made its way across the entire plaza. "This is Father Valenta. The meeting is over. Go home."

No one was listening. Just as he disappeared inside, the main door gave way at last. The tide of people surged in, hesitated, and continued, pushed by the weight of people behind. People squirmed in at windows like worms. Space opened up in the plaza, between onlookers and rioters.

"Is it over?" asked Tim. "Can we go home now?"

"You can," said Nan. "I've got to find out what happened with Persh and Big Daddy."

She slid off the wall and helped him down after her. Suddenly the mob surged back from the doors. She shoved him behind her. What if the police retreat had been a trap, and the rioters were running out, blind with tear gas, trampling the people behind them? Glass continued to break loudly as the PA system came to life again. "All right, people, listen to me!" The new voice crackled like burning leaves, and the pudgy man waved his arms from the steps. "I told Mr. Maverick we didn't want Communism, Fascism, Nazism, or any other un-American creeds in San Antonio!"

Applause rose like thunder from the plaza, drowning what came next. The rioters had taken over the building! Tim gripped Nan's hand painfully and damply as the loudspeakers squeaked and clattered about Americanism and a new rally. Without meaning to, they began moving forward—running forward—shoved ahead by yet more people materializing behind them. It might have been

Nan's imagination that she saw, before the wall of grown-ups blocked her view entirely, Big Daddy among those waving a flag above the speaker's head.

Nan tried to push her way across the shoving, trampling crowd. At last they staggered out of the mainstream and nearly fell in the flower beds beside the steps. They sat on the ground, gasping for breath. Nan was certain she had skinned her knee, and tried to concentrate on that.

"Hey, you kids all right?" asked a mild, familiar voice behind them.

Nan almost screamed; the voice was so well known, and so unexpected. Persh stood between them and the madly hurrying feet, his camera swinging from his neck. "I'm —I'm okay."

"We thought we saw you get hit with a rock," said Tim, looking up at him in eager relief.

Persh shook his head. "I think that was somebody from a newspaper. Didn't Mr. Chadwell warn y'all to stay away?"

"He warned you, too," said Nan. In the semidarkness he was more clearly Grampa; but he was a Grampa who didn't know them, who ran with mobs that shouted at people to kill policemen, and she couldn't deal with it. She stood up and almost shouted at him. "What are you doing here? What's anybody doing here? Why would anybody do all this? It's awful, awful, awful, awful, *awful*!"

"Yes it is," said Persh, in Grampa's voice; and at the sound Nan knew that if she tried to speak again, she'd cry. So she didn't speak, leaving Tim to ask the important question:

"Did you throw rocks?"

"No, I didn't," he answered sadly, "but I didn't stop anybody from throwing any, and I wish I hadn't come."

Nan swallowed. She couldn't let Tim do all the work while she fell apart. "What—what was it all about, anyway? What had the people inside done?"

"They didn't have much chance to do anything," said Persh. "Do you know what a Communist is?"

Nan nodded.

"Well, that's what the people inside were. This woman named Emma Tenayuca Brooks got a permit to have a Communist meeting here, and people—didn't like it."

"But—you've got to let people have meetings," said Nan.

"Yes. But practically nobody—except Mr. Maverick, the mayor—he gave them the permit—thought we ought to let them have the meeting here. This is our Memorial Auditorium, you know, dedicated to men who died fighting to make the world safe for democracy. They thought a Communist meeting would be insulting to their memory. Communists are against democracy, you know."

The PA system was barking again, but Nan didn't listen, looking around at the crushed flowers and the gaps of fresh dirt where bricks lining the flower bed had been torn up.

"Did Mr. Maverick and the Communists get away?" asked Tim, in a small voice.

"Oh, yes. I don't think Mr. Maverick even showed up, and the police got all the people at the meeting out before they abandoned the building. Don't you worry about that."

Nan took a deep breath. She had to know. "What about Mr. Chadwell? Where's he?"

Persh looked surprised. "Oh, he's at the Americanism rally. I think he was one of the people carrying the flag from the room the Communists were going to use. He'll be here for a while. But it's high time y'all went home."

Tim looked at Nan, and said, hesitantly, "We're staying at that hotel over there. We'll be fine."

"I ought to walk you back over there," said Persh, checking his watch, "but if I don't hurry I'm going to miss my bus. You sure you're okay?"

"We're fine," said Nan, brushing herself off, and extending a hand to get Tim to his feet. "Just fine, thank you."

Her voice must have sounded better to him than to her, because he walked into the darkness and left them there. Crowds milled around still, at the doors of the Auditorium and around the edges of the plaza—spectators robbed of spectacle, undecided whether to stay or go, or take part in the Americanism rally. Nan led Tim around back of the building, where the shattered windshields of closely packed parked cars glittered in stray reflections.

"I wish we hadn't come," said Tim.

"It's too late now," said Nan crossly. "Let's go home."

They turned their backs on the Auditorium, facing the black abyss of the river beyond the parking lot, and wished to go home.

15

The Disputed Stump

T he pace of the days quickened as Gramma started a long list of projects she was determined to get done before school began. When Nan had first read *Jane Eyre*, it had taken two days and left her giddy. Now, when she wanted to reread it, she was continually interrupted—by trips to pick out patterns and fabrics for school clothes; by sightseeing trips and visits to obscure relatives; by the rearrangement of the photographs on the wall, packing away some that had been out and hanging ones that had been packed away. Gramma had suddenly got tired of the way the walls looked. Livvy's friend Margie came back from camp, and she and Nan liked each other. The three of them decided to go out for something together when school started, like choir or gymnastics or basketball, and discussed their merits endlessly while walking to the Y and during TV commercials.

The *Spirit of the Place* picture now hung over Nan's bed

as a sort of conscience. Tim had acquired a set of small pictures, overlapping in one large frame like a montage, depicting the house in various stages of recovery from the flood. Grampa had not taken them, of course, only redis-covered them and put them together in chronological or-der. Tim studied them as if they were a treasure map.

Nan continued working the site methodically, an hour or so early every morning, and sometimes Livvy and Margie wanted to look for arrowheads. Though her enthusiasm for time traveling had been dampened by the riot, Nan felt she had to get as much digging done as possible. By the time Mom and Dad came home next spring, she wanted a complete and testable Theory of Time Travel worked out. It helped that Mom and Dad were interested in her progress, and always asked about her finds in their letters. Their own dig was going well. They had found a potter's garbage dump, and were having a wonderful time.

While she dug neat squares and charted the locations of bottle caps, Tim mooned around, reading, scribbling poetry, or playing with the cat—until a sudden frenzy seized him, and he lit into the creek bank with the vigor of a dog digging after a rabbit. He put aches in his back, blisters on his fingers, and sunburn on his nose. He un-covered a few artifacts (put back for later experimentation, like those Nan was finding), but he seemed to know exactly what he was looking for, and took no interest in anything else.

It occurred to Nan that Margie and Livvy would be

more fun to time travel with than he was, so she introduced them to the idea, pretending it was a game, and they tried it with one of the bonfire artifacts. This led to one last big pretend game before giving up such childishness in seventh grade. They recited Nan's poem over one of the bonfire artifacts, and played a really neat make-believe adventure. But it was only a game. Nan wondered if the talent was specific to her family; or if the travelers had to be related to the person who had used the artifact. There wasn't any good way to tell.

Bob and Stella and Aunt Faith came to supper one night, and Nan cooked for them, Gramma sitting on the kitchen stool in front of the fan and directing. It was only spaghetti, salad, and garlic bread; but Nan tasted the result with satisfaction. The others were surprised and complimentary. "You ought to have Nan cook more often," Bob said. "You deserve the rest."

Gramma snorted. "If you had your way I'd sit in a chair with my hands folded all day. I don't work anything like as hard as my mama did. Why, I don't remember her ever doing less than two things at once. Knitting and reading and watching the kids while she waited for the Sunday roast to cook, that's how I remember her. The day she died, she raked the yard, baked cookies, finished her quilt, put beans on to soak, and said she felt good because she'd gotten stuff done. Went to bed bone tired, and slept herself straight into death. That's how I'd like to go—fall asleep after a good day's work, and just keep sleeping."

Nan's spine felt cold. "Gramma, can we make fudge tomorrow?" she asked abruptly.

"Oh, land! It's too hot for fudge. How about brownies?"

It was hot, of course—so hot that the chocolate squares, which had been kept in the pantry, melted faster than the refrigerated butter when they made brownies next morning. Still, after the incredible July heat, the mid-nineties were cool enough for Tim to tackle the creek bank. The brownies were baking, Nan was wiping the counters, and Gramma was washing the chocolate out of the saucepan, when he cried out, "I found it! I found it!"

"Found what?" called Gramma through the window.

"The flood tree! Come look!"

"Coming." Gramma wiped her hands on her apron and set the timer on the windowsill so they'd hear it.

Tim had left the confines of the garden, digging up the bank in what would have been squares 5N7E and 4N7E if Nan had staked that far. A rusty knitting needle, the fragile bones of a small animal, a can, and a strip of rubber were laid out in a row with the notebook, but Tim was vigorously whipping the dirt from something still below ground level. "I bet you haven't been making drawings of where you found these things," said Nan accusingly.

"Oh, I did, too! I'll show you later. Come look at this!"

"We're going to have to put all this dirt back," said Gramma, sternly. "I don't want my yard eroding. What happened to just digging the garden?"

"I could tell I wasn't going to find it there." Tim stood

back so they could see his find—a large, dark lump, half buried still, with haphazard protrusions at the bottom.

Nan looked at it, walked around to get a different angle, and looked some more. "What is it?"

"It's the tree stump, dummy."

"Don't you call your sister names," said Gramma.

Nan looked again. "Okay, it's a tree stump. So?"

"It's *the* tree stump," said Tim impatiently. "The stump of the tree that saved Gramma in the flood."

"Oh, now, I don't think that's very likely, sugar," said Gramma. "That tree tore up by the roots and washed away."

"I'm sure this is the one," said Tim. "I bet it broke off when it fell over, and after it started floating, the root part just sank. I feel in my bones this is the right one."

Gramma laughed. "I'm afraid your bones are a bit young to be trustworthy yet. It may have washed there during the flood, though, I guess."

"Anyway, I can't dig it up myself."

"You don't need to dig it up at all."

"But it has to go in the collection."

"I'll get the camera and take some pictures, but that'll have to do. I'm not having that dirty big thing in my sewing room."

"We can clean it," Tim protested, but Gramma was firm.

Nan didn't blame her. "It's just too big," she said, when they washed up before tackling the warm brownies

147

with ice cream. "It wouldn't fit in the apartment when we go home, and there isn't any good place to put it even here. The rest of the stuff you found's good, though. We might be able to go somewhere with the knitting needle. Why don't we ask Gramma where it might have come from, and see if we can get a poem?"

"I don't want to make poems about any dumb old knitting needle," said Tim.

He mooned around the rest of the day. Gramma let them off filling in the bank till the next morning, as the temperature rose, and Livvy, Margie, and one of Livvy's brother's came to take them swimming. In the evening, Nan helped with dinner, pumping Gramma about the needle while scraping carrots.

Apparently Great-Gramma had liked to knit and mend outdoors, where she got the full breeze and could watch her kids. Nan hadn't thought much about Great-Gramma before, but as Gramma talked about her now, she began to look forward to meeting her. Great-Gramma had sung show tunes and made all the family's clothes; fixed the girls' hair in the latest styles right here in the kitchen; kept chickens, which she hated, right up to the end of the war and the advance of the city into the neighborhood; held dances in the living room; never raised her voice. Nan started trying to think of rhymes for *needle*.

They had been sleeping upstairs again since the nighttime temperatures had become bearable. The upper floor was dark and quiet when Nan came up after kissing

Gramma good night; just the night light low in the hall, the sound of Gramma running the downstairs tub, and the buzzing of the fan in Tim's room.

"Hey! Nan!" Tim's white, heaped shape leaned toward the door from the foot of his bed.

"What's the matter?" Nan whispered. "Why aren't you asleep?"

"I'm not going to sleep. I'm going to the flood."

He sat cross-legged, Satchmo tucked in the hollows of his knees, his pajama top off. He looked young, incompetent, and eager. "What do you want to go to the flood for?" whispered Nan. "You'd get yourself drowned."

"No, I wouldn't! You know we can go home whenever we want."

"We think we can. Why do you want to go there, anyway?"

"Because I'm Utnapishtim," he explained, as if it should be self-evident. "Anyway, we were there. We must've been the kids in the tree. So we have to go."

"We don't have to do anything," Nan informed him. "What makes you think we're the kids in the tree?"

"Where else would they come from, if this house was in the country then? If they'd been neighbors, Gramma'd've said. It makes sense."

"It does not. Anyway, I don't want to go to any flood."

"I helped you go to the bonfire when I didn't want to go."

"It probably isn't even the right tree."

149

"I'm sure it is. And I made my best poem ever."

"Well—let me think about it."

"She'll make us bury the stump again tomorrow. This is the only chance we'll get."

Nan chewed her lip. It was obviously a stupid idea to go to a flood, but Tim was so eager and determined she felt mean saying no. Besides, it probably wouldn't work. "Okay. Tell you what. Wait till Gramma goes to bed, and then come get me. We'll need to take slickers in case you're right, and"—this should settle it!—"I don't think we should go downstairs. Gramma'd be sure to hear us. We'll have to climb down the pecan tree."

Tim swallowed. "I can—I can do that."

"In the dark? You sure?"

"Yeah. Yeah, I'm sure. If that's the only way to do it."

Nan went to bed feeling she had done well. Gramma didn't go to bed till after ten. Tim would never stay awake that long. She was surprised when he dumped a slicker on her dozing dreams and hissed, "Aren't you ready yet?"

"Give me a minute! I was just resting! What're you doing in your pajamas still?"

"We've got to look like flood victims."

"Nobody'll see under the slicker. Go get dressed—and tiptoe!"

He vanished quietly. Uneasily, Nan donned jeans and a T-shirt, socks, and tennis shoes. Big Daddy's eyes seemed to follow her from the picture above her bed. "I've got to

150

be fair to Tim," she explained to him. "I've also got to stop being so bossy. So what can I do?"

Big Daddy didn't answer. She turned her back on him.

For a minute she hoped Tim was going to chicken out of climbing down the tree, and then she hoped the scrambling noise he made getting from window to branch would wake Gramma; but under her guidance he got down all right, landing more or less unscathed, and pleased with himself. "See. I'm braver'n you think I am."

"You don't know what I think," whispered Nan, dropping the bundle of slickers out of the tree, and herself after them. "Come on. Nothing's going to happen, so let's get it over with."

Their eyes had adjusted to the dark, and no clouds covered the moon, so they had no difficulty finding the gaping black hole in the bank. "Okay," said Nan, pulling her slicker on. "Let's hear this fabulous poem of yours."

Tim cleared his throat.

> "I am Utnapishtim,
> descendant of the flood.
> The memory of the water
> is flowing in my blood.
>
> The live oak tree that saved us
> was broken by the stream;
> the stump remaining only
> now that water seems a dream.

I was there. I wasn't born yet.
I was there, though, all the same;
and I will be there this evening.
Utnapishtim is my name."

Nan sweated under her slicker. "That'll probably work for you," she said, "but what about me?"

"Oh, I'll hang onto you. And you know it only works for both of us. You ready?"

"For anything," she said, glumly.

They joined their left hands, right hands on the rough gritty surface of the stump, and chanted the poem softly, in unison. Nan substituted second person for first throughout. "Nothing'll happen, anyway," she told herself, watching Tim's rapt face—eyes closed, pale in the moonlight. For the first time she wondered who in the family Tim took after. She took inventory as she chanted, finding bits of Dad, and Grampa, and Mom, and Aunt Marian, and —how odd! Now she thought about it, when his hair was wet, it was just the same color as Big Daddy's slicked-back hair had been at the riot. His face began to break up into its component parts—the world was whirling, shifting, breaking up as her body rippled. And the rain dumped on top of her, pouring down the neck of her slicker.

16
Many Waters

*N*an gripped the sturdy roots of the tree, now standing tall, as the water seized her shoulders and tried to drag her away. Tim's squeal was barely audible over the roar of the flood and a grumble of thunder. "Climb, you dummy, climb!" she shouted, struggling to pull herself out of the creek. The bank slid dangerously under her feet, but with the help of the tree she made it. On hands and knees, she felt around the tree's roots till she found Tim's desperately clutching hand, and dragged him up beside her.

"I knew it!" he crowed, through streams of water running from his hair, nose, and glasses. "I knew it, I knew it! Didn't I tell you this was the right tree?"

"Okay. You're right. Let's go home now." Nan scrambled to her feet, and helped Tim up, too. The wind drove the rain into her face like millions of tiny needles. Water foamed around the tree roots and her shoe soles. She couldn't see across the creek at all, just water, below and above, as far as she could see, even when lightning flashed distantly. The house was shadowy under the rain, a colorless hulk, unlit, apparently unliving.

"Don't be a dweeb!" said Tim. "We've got to climb this tree and be the kids in the story."

"No, we don't. We can go home and see if our not being here changes the story any. It's important to know if it's possible to change history, if you're going to time travel."

Nan thought this a good argument as she said it, but Tim saw through her at once. "You're just chicken! You can go home if you want, but I'm going to be here for the story!"

"Don't be dumb! You know you can't climb a tree without me." The water was over her ankles, soaking her tennis shoes from inside as well as out. Tim's arms were folded stubbornly. Nan growled and gave up. "C'mon. I'll give you a boost."

The water rose all the time he scaled the trunk, settled on a broad branch, and leaned to help her up beside him. Among the close-packed oval leaves, the rain was less fierce; but every gust of wind reduced their protection. Their slickers ran like fountains. Lightning flashed again, but it seemed to be heading away from them, while the water was visibly rising. Anyway, they knew this tree didn't get hit by lightning. Nan led Tim further up, the bark dis-

154

gustingly soft and wet under her bare hands. The world stank wetly. They found seats in view of the house. Nan shielded her eyes, hanging on with her legs and one hand. "The water's at the foundation," she shouted. "Our pecan tree's gone!"

"Isn't there yet, you mean!" Tim corrected, as primly as he could at the top of his lungs.

"You know what I mean." Nan wiped futilely at the water on her face. "So what now?"

"Now we wait for the story to start," said Tim, taking off his glasses and sticking them in his slicker pocket.

"You better snap that shut," said Nan. "If this is the story, we have to fall in the water sometime."

Tim obeyed. Dogs barked somewhere, nearly inaudible in the racket. Nan was cold, and getting colder. They might as well have come in their pajamas, for all the good the jeans and slickers had done them. The world was made of different shades of darkness, so that it was hard to track the progress of the flood up the sides of the house, or even to see Tim clearly. She could feel him shivering, crouching nearer and nearer to her as the wind stripped the leaves away. "Stop crowding," she said. "You can't see anything, anyway."

"I can see okay," said Tim. "Better than I did before I took my glasses off. I think the water's to the porch now."

Nan was inclined to agree with him; but the wind at that moment seized the tree and shook it, as if they were ripe acorns it wanted to shake down. Nan grabbed onto Tim's slicker with her free hand. "Whatever you do, don't let go!"

"I know!" he snapped.

She could tell he was beginning to be scared. Well, good! It served him right. Nan gritted her teeth to keep them from hitting against each other.

It seemed to her that the racket of the flood changed subtly, and streaks of white appeared on the house—water foaming in at cracks and crevices, at windowpanes and door frames Big Daddy had made as solid and draftproof as he could. Chickens began cackling frantically, and a nearby dog began to bark—a clear, ringing sound that pierced the other noises better than a siren.

A tiny light came on in the house, unnaturally bright and painful. It wasn't shaped right for a flashlight, but it moved. Nan had a hard time tracking it—Gramma's room—bathroom—no, that couldn't be the bathroom. Then a hole full of light opened in the wall, and they saw Big Daddy, huge and bright with a lantern in his hand, trying to wade out the door against the surge of water around his knees. The wind tore the screen door till it drooped and slid sideways. Big Daddy staggered, shouting unintelligibly. A second light appeared on the second floor—Nan's room. Big Daddy struggled to close the door, but the inrushing flood was too strong. Oily rainbows flashed on the surface as his light wavered in his hand. Nan turned away her dazzled eyes, blinking, and saw a

156

white shape skimming on the surface of the water, smaller white shapes spilling from it like Kleenex from a full wastebasket.

She had barely realized that the chicken coop was washing away, when the light lessened, and a thump shook the tree. She turned her head in time to see a dark, unrecognizable shape whirl away on the current. Big Daddy had given up on the door and retreated inside again. Soon the upstairs windows brightened.

Nan remembered a fever she had had once, in which time stretched and distorted like Silly Putty, and dreams came, but sleep did not. This was like that, only cold—the movement of vague shapes beyond the curtains, the ruthlessly rising water, the vanishing lightning, the objects tumbling recklessly toward them. The tree began to take a beating, as boards and tires, doors and boxes, branches and bedsprings, hurtled down from upstream. Nan and Tim climbed higher. A baby cried, but the dog ceased to bark. A huge thing like a tent wrapped itself around the tree as if clinging for dear life; but in time the flood snatched it away with a tremendous ripping sound.

"I wish they'd get to the roof!" complained Tim through shaking teeth.

"We don't have to stay here!"

"Yes we do! We're in the story!" He didn't sound happy about it anymore.

Nan wondered if she could jerk him back, as he had jerked her back that first time. If she failed, though, he'd be here alone. Maybe that would make him see sense. What if he didn't follow her? Would she be able to come after him? If only she knew where to find a second flood relic!

The people inside pushed something large and awkward out the side window where the pecan should be. They could hear Big Daddy shouting, but couldn't make out the words. "What are they doing?" asked Tim.

"How do I know?" Nan watched intently. A few more things came out; then a figure that could only be Big Daddy, balancing on the sill and tugging at a line around his waist—nearly invisible against the light.

"But—that roof's not wide enough! They'll fall in if they sit there!" protested Tim.

Nan didn't answer, watching the movements of the dark figure in the dark rain. He braced himself on all fours on the narrow roof and began moving one distorted hand up and down. Bang! Bang! It took Nan a minute to figure out what this meant, but when she did, it seemed obvious. "He's building the raft!" she shouted.

"Already? They aren't lined up on the roof like drowned pigeons yet!"

Nan didn't answer, busy comparing reality with Gramma's story. Now she thought of it, several things didn't look right. This tree was too small, for one thing. If the water got high enough that the family had to climb onto the roof of the second story, she and Tim would drown.

And how was the family supposed to get up there, anyway? She hadn't realized it before, but the attic windows were way too small for a grown-up to fit through. Nan gave up on the idea of dragging Tim back to their own time—though she knew, as a china cabinet thudded against the tree and the branches groaned and swayed beneath her, that she ought to do it.

The noise of the flood must've drowned the singing of "Papa Gonna Buy You a Mockingbird." They only heard "Rock of Ages" because Big Daddy sang it, too, in a strong voice full of gaps and bad notes, as he swung his hammer. The voices of the others were barely audible.

"May the water and the blood," sang Tim, sounding cracked and breathless.

"From his wounded side that flowed," Nan joined in, sounding no better.

> "Be of sin the double cure;
> Save from wrath, and make me pure!"

She felt better, singing—or maybe it was just that she was losing the feeling in her arms and legs. The people in the house seemed closer than they had a minute ago.

The next song was "A Mighty Fortress Is Our God," to which neither Nan nor Tim knew the words very well. They limped and stumbled through it as best they could, unnoticed. However, when Big Daddy—apparently pick-

159

ing up on the faint sounds indoors—swung into the middle of the first line of "Swing Low, Sweet Chariot," they were able to belt the words out with confidence and volume. It had been one of Tim's class's songs in the end-of-school program last year, and he had gone around practicing it till Nan had longed to tape his mouth shut. Now she was just glad she knew the words so well. At the chorus, Big Daddy raised his head and fell silent, leaving their voices to combat the flood alone. "Who's there?" he called. "Where are you?"

"In your tree!" hollered Nan, getting a mouthful of rain.

"You all right?"

"Just fine!" bellowed Tim.

A huge shape whirled past Big Daddy, to disintegrate into a mess of boards against the tree even as he shouted: "Look out!" Nan gasped and clung tighter, unable to respond before his second anxious call.

"Don't worry about us! We're okay!"

"How many of you are there?"

"Two!"

"I'm making a raft here!" Gramma had been right; he did have a voice like a bull. "High ground's not a quarter-mile away, if we can beat the current! As soon as it's ready, we'll come after you!" He stuck his head back into the window, talking with the people inside; then pulled out again. "Can you keep singing?"

160

"As long as you can!" Tim answered.

After a while they ran out of hymns. They were singing "Polly Wolly Doodle," a great deal of raft stuck off the edge of the roof, and the water was less than a foot below the window, when a whirling shed shot into sight and barreled into the raft. Knocked loose, the raft hurtled into the water, and so did Big Daddy.

Nan and Tim had not finished their astonished screams when the shed smashed into the tree and disintegrated into boards. The trunk groaned, and—Nan thought—shifted on its roots. Someone was leaning out the window, hauling at the line, disappearing back inside as Big Daddy clambered back onto the roof. He stumbled against the window, and remained there a minute. He's safe! thought Nan, relaxing inside. "It's a good thing he was tied to the house," she said aloud. "He must be hugging Great-Gramma through the window."

"Y'all okay?" he called toward them.

"Yes, sir!"

"Just sit tight! We'll think of something!"

Uncle Will Wright had better come soon, thought Nan. Oily rainbows swirled on water perilously close to her window. She did not like to think how near the flood was to their own numb feet. Instead she began to sing the first song that came into her head. She was halfway through the first chorus before she realized that it was the song they'd sung at Grampa's funeral.

"Shall we gather at the river?
The beautiful, the beautiful river?"

Big Daddy was straddling the windowsill, ready to go in, when she saw the light bobbing unsteadily toward them. Tim was the one who shouted, "Look behind you!"

Big Daddy looked. "Will!" he roared. "Just the man I wanted to see!"

They couldn't hear the answer; but they saw the rowboat struggle across the current, saw Big Daddy crawl down the roof again to draw it in with his hands and hold it while they tossed in a line. The boat turned round in the current till it bumped the eaves. Big Daddy was gesturing, the boaters gabbling and moving their heads. Nan shifted on the branch, feeling the bark crumble under her as she tried to shake feeling into her foot.

A new figure came to the window—too short for a grown-up, too tall for any of the children. That'll be Polly the baby-sitter, thought Nan, as Big Daddy helped her into the boat. It and the lantern in its bow waved dangerously; but the boaters did something with their oars, and all settled down safely. Then a small figure was passed out, from window, to Big Daddy, to boatman, to Polly. That's Great-Aunt Becky, Nan thought, flexing her hands. We're almost done. She could feel a new tension across her shoulders.

A larger child was passed out—Great-Uncle Jake. Big Daddy leaned in the window again. "This is it," hissed
162

Nan. Tim moaned softly. She thought he said, "I can't look!"

The bundle of Gramma passed from Great-Gramma to Big Daddy.

Big Daddy held her out. A boatman leaned over the bulwark.

The boat swung and lifted as something thudded against it, and Gramma fell.

Everyone screamed but Nan and Big Daddy, who was in the water, swimming furiously, brought up short by his safety line.

The shapeless, howling lump hurtled toward the tree, right behind the piano stool (piano stool?) that had struck the boat.

Nan was already in the water, but not in quite the right place. Her thrashing arms found the edge of a baby blanket, and she hauled in on it—feeling it begin to unwrap itself. She kicked off her shoes and stroked with one arm, so cold she barely felt Gramma even when she got a grip on her. Twigs and branches slapped at her and vanished. The water was in her nose, and her eyes, and she couldn't even try to swim, not and hold the baby clear of the water. She had been so stupid to jump in. Her slicker had caught on the outermost twigs, but soon it would have to come loose, and then the weight would drag her under.

Something stronger than the current tugged at the slicker, something she could work with instead of against. Nan was not surprised to find Big Daddy pulling her back into the shelter of the tree, holding on with both legs and hauling. "I got her!" she gasped, as he pulled her against his chest. "I almost didn't but I got her!"

"Good girl! Up you go!" She had to climb up him to get back into the tree beside a ghostly white Tim. Big Daddy's cut safety line trailed behind him like a tail as he climbed after her. She handed him the baby. The dog howled—had been howling—and the baby screamed in a hideous pulsing rhythm louder than the flood. Nan coughed greasy-tasting water and blinked anxiously, trying to determine whether or not she still had her contacts. Big Daddy cradled the baby and made incongruous shushing sounds. Tim shrieked in Nan's ear, "Look out!"

Nan looked up in time to see an upright piano smash into the trunk and closed her eyes against the uprush of water as the tree, tired of its long battering, gave way before the force of the blow.

"Now, Tim, now!" she shouted, fighting her way to the surface. Two strokes would have reached the whirling tree, but her arms and legs were too dead to make them.

"Grab my line!" shouted Big Daddy, still clinging to the treetop and the baby. Nan could see the light of the boat bearing down on them.

"Home!" shouted Tim, spitting water. "Home!" To Big Daddy it must have looked as if the flood swallowed him, but Nan saw him ripple out of existence.

Big Daddy was shouting, but her ears were under water, and she could barely see anything, keeping her eyes half shut so she wouldn't lose her contacts. Home, she thought, knowing everyone was safe now. The boat was right on top of Big Daddy. It would pick him up, and that would be different from the story, too—

Nan saw him thrust Gramma into a pair of arms reaching out of the boat; saw him let go of the upholding, spinning tree; saw him swimming like a human wave toward her free-floating body, coming to rescue her. But she couldn't let him do that. She squeezed her eyes tight shut, and longed for home with all her might.

17

The Sleep of the Just

*F*or a moment she hung terrifyingly in empty space; then she was falling; then she was just pain, without enough air in her to scream. When she could think again, she thought maybe she was drowning, but then her memory revived. This was how it had felt the time she'd fallen off the jungle gym and knocked the wind out of herself. She had to have been twelve feet off the ground in that flood! More, if she had happened to be over the creek bed. She'd be lucky if she—if neither of them—broke anything.

The night was clear, gray, and welcomingly warm. Someone revved a motorcycle. Wind rattled leaves faintly. They were in the yard of the house directly across the alley, next door to Livvy. Nan was crushing a geranium bed, while Tim was curled up a few feet away on a compost heap. What if one of them had landed on a fence, or a rosebush? Why didn't Tim move?

Nan crawled toward him, water shaking from her slicker with each movement. When she got close, she could hear him making thin, shaky, gulping sounds. She touched his wet hair. "Tim? You okay? You hurt anywhere?"

He looked up, his face streaked black and white. "I d-didn't do anyth-thing!"

"Nobody said you did. You okay?"

"N-no! I m-mean—" He sat up, holding her hands too tightly. "I s-saw Gramma fall, and-d I saw you go aft-ter her, and I s-saw B-Big Daddy go after y-you and I ju-ju-just s-sat there!"

He was crying so hard he was barely breathing. Nan couldn't do anything but hug him, muffling the sound against her chest. They needed to get out of here before their noise woke anyone. "There wasn't anything for you to do," she said. "Come on. Everything's fine now."

"If it'd ju-just been m-me there, Gramma would've died!"

It was a sobering thought, but Nan didn't think she believed it. "Well, but she didn't die! Can you stand up?"

Walking on their stiff and bloodless legs was almost impossible. When the blood returned, they had to sit down and gasp in agony a few times till the pins and needles passed. It didn't help that Nan's tennis shoes were nearly seventy years away and she had to cross the alley in her sock feet. Nan didn't want to climb the pecan tree in their current state, and had hopes of the open lower windows; but she couldn't pry the screens loose. She climbed up the

167

tree, then, making the trip from branch to window on sheer determination, and came down to let Tim in the back door. It seemed to her they made a lot of noise. She kept listening for Gramma to demand what they were doing running around in the middle of the night.

They were both filthy, covered with the grease that had made the rainbows in the water. Only very thorough, very hot showers could have restored them; and they were just too tired to take them. In the end Nan spread towels all over their beds and tucked Tim in on his. Every towel in the upstairs bathroom would be dirty come morning, but Nan didn't see what she could do about it. At least they went to bed mostly dry.

"What're we going to tell Gramma?" she asked herself, but fell asleep before she had time to frame an answer.

Satchmo woke her by walking on her face—something he had never done to her before. Nan rolled over and pushed him away, crying out at the pain in her arm. Satchmo patted her face imperiously with his sheathed paw. The room was already light. Nan put on her glasses to read the clock—seven-thirty. That wasn't near enough sleep. She tried to get comfortable again, but she was too sore.

Well, there was no point antagonizing Gramma straight off. She would listen better to an early riser than to a lazybones, and, once Gramma understood, Nan could get rubbed all over with Ben-Gay, and take a nap.

Nan realized that, at some point during the night, she

had decided that it was time to tell the grown-ups. Time travel was just too dangerous to keep a secret with Tim anymore. She would write to Mom and Dad today, but she would also have to tell Gramma, and the sooner she got started cleaning up the mess they had made, the less trouble she'd be in.

She looked in on Tim on her way to the bathroom. He had shoved half the towels off the bed, and was curled up in the remaining ones, snoring slightly. Probably his nose was stopped up. Nan felt a little stuffy herself. She scrubbed herself hard in the shower, using the hottest water she could bear. When she got out, clean and sore, she found Satchmo running up and down the stairs, lashing his tail and mewing crossly. "What's the matter with you?"

"Mrar!" complained Satchmo.

Downstairs, she could hear the fan buzzing in the master bedroom, and various noises from outdoors. Satchmo's food bowl was empty, and cat hair floated on the surface of his water. A pot was on the stove. Nan looked inside, finding that Gramma had put black-eyed peas on to soak. The coffee machine was empty, and the counter ashtray clean. Eight o'clock, and Gramma not up yet! Nan fed the cat with murmurs of delayed sympathy, and considered what kind of breakfast she was capable of cooking.

The fried eggs got kind of dark on the bottom, the bacon took longer and came out crisper than she'd planned, and the Cream of Wheat just wouldn't thicken. She knew the coffee would be drinkable, because she'd often made

169

it at home for Mom and Dad. Satchmo was licking his whiskers on the back steps, the table was set, the orange juice was poured, and still she was alone. Nan began to feel anxious. Suppose—she didn't see quite how, but what if being tossed in the flood as a baby last night had affected Gramma as a grown lady this morning?

Nan went to the master bedroom, walking softly on bare feet. The door stood open. The fan buzzed. The curtains breathed against the window as the air flowed in and out. Gramma lay on her side, one bare arm on top of the sheet, the other propping up the pillow. Cat hairs darkened the sheet. "Gramma? Gramma, it's time to get up." Nan touched her shoulder.

Gramma's skin was cooler than the air around it, stiff, and dry, and pale, like paper.

"Gramma!" Nan shook her, and the shaking didn't feel right. Gramma's eyelids didn't flutter. She did not roll over, mumbling and smacking her lips. She did not breathe.

Nan ran around the bed and snatched up the receiver on the old black phone. The dial turned impossibly slowly under her frantic fingers. The emergency operator's voice was reassuringly calm. "Are you alone there?" she asked, when Nan had gulped out her problem.

"Me and my little brother."

"Okay. I'll send someone right over. You shut your Gramma's room—don't let your little brother in there—

and get hold of a neighbor or somebody to come be with you. What's your address?"

Nan gave it. Before she left the room she looked at Gramma, still lying in the same position. She felt her throat close up. Walking softly—as softly as Satchmo— she shut the door behind her and went to the kitchen phone. All Gramma's important numbers were written on a pad on the wall beside it. Bob and Stella were medical people. They'd know what to do. They'd be able to explain this to Tim. Her hand shook as she dialed their number.

18
Circles

*D*ad didn't look like himself in the charcoal gray suit he had gotten for Grampa's funeral and had never worn since. Mom's black dress made her look too pale. They had gotten in from the Mideast late last night and had slept on the Hide-A-Bed at Aunt Faith's while Nan and Tim were bundled onto cots in the sewing room there.

The house had been empty since the morning Nan and Tim had left in Stella's car, leaving Gramma cold and quiet on her bed. It felt different now—stuffy from being shut up, crowded with mourners, humid with tears. Nan kept expecting to step on Satchmo, though she knew perfectly well he was safe at Stella's apartment.

"So you're Nan," said a young woman with a familiar voice, whom Stella introduced as Cousin Mary Beth. "It must have been so awful for you, finding her like that!"

A lot of people had told Nan that today. She still hadn't thought of a good response. She mumbled something and excused herself, only realizing in the midst of her escape why the voice sounded familiar. She looked over her shoulder, and compared sight with memory. Cousin Mary Beth was like the oldest girl at Mom and Dad's wedding. She was about the right age now, too. Suddenly Nan wanted something to eat very badly.

The dining room table was packed with hams, beans, potato salads, Jell-O molds—all the cold food people had brought. Nan filled one plate for herself, and one for Tim, then wandered around till she found him slumped on the back steps. "I'm not hungry," he mumbled, not looking at her.

"Eat anyway," Nan commanded. "Gramma'd want you to."

He sighed, took a forkful of potato salad, grimaced, and ate. Nan ate also, hearing the meaningless mumble of the people in the kitchen blending into the meaningless chatter of the locusts in the yard. She tried to think about Gramma and Grampa's reunion in heaven, but she couldn't picture it. Did they have kitchens in heaven? If so, who did the dishes? It was hard to think of Gramma as a soul, detached from cigarettes and soups.

"You think she called for us while we were at the flood?" asked Tim.

"No, I don't," said Nan, more firmly than she felt. "The doctor said she never woke up. I bet she was—I bet it happened before we left. Otherwise she'd've heard us in the pecan tree."

"If I'd done something when Gramma fell in the water—"

"It's not your fault!"

"What's not his fault?" asked Dad, sitting down beside her.

Nan jumped guiltily. She had never written her letter about time travel, but had spent a lot of the week, when she wasn't trying to read *Jane Eyre* or the Gospel of John, composing the explanation in her head. She still didn't know how to start, even if this were a good time—and she didn't think it was. Mom sat down next to Tim, looking fragile and tired. Nan tried to keep her voice casual. "Oh, he's being a worrywart."

"I am not," said Tim. "I just wonder."

"Wonder about what?" asked Mom.

"If we could've done something." Tim glared at Nan. "You said you were going to tell them."

"There's plenty of time."

"Tell us what?" asked Dad.

"That we weren't in bed the night she died," said Nan, reluctantly. "We climbed out the tree by my window."

"It was my idea," Tim put in.

"I could've made you stay."

"Could not!"

"It's a bit late for that now," said Mom. "Where'd you go?"

Tim made an uncertain motion with his hands.

"Some place she'd told you not to go?" prompted Dad.

"Well—she didn't know we could get there," said Nan. "But she would've told us not to if she knew—only it turned out to be a good thing—only—I wish we hadn't done it that night."

"We had to do it sooner or later," said Tim. "And that was our only chance."

Mom and Dad looked anything but enlightened. Dad stood up. "Why don't we go for a walk and you can tell us all about it?"

"Um—why don't we show you the dig first?" Nan suggested. "It's part of the story."

The site looked forlorn already. Mom and Dad admired Nan's neat squares, and waited patiently while she pointed out the locations of important artifacts. The bank had not been filled in yet, and the stump was dry and rotting in the sun. "Remember the tree in the story about the flood?" asked Tim. "This is it."

"It can't be," said Mom. "That tree got uprooted."

"Well—not really," said Nan. "See, Gramma couldn't remember for herself, and the story got changed. I mean —it was almost seventy years ago! And nobody saw the whole thing clearly anyway. What really happened was, a piano came down on the flood, and hit the tree, and broke it."

"How do you know?"

"We were there," said Tim. "Nan saved Gramma's life, and then Big Daddy saved them both. And I just sat there!"

Mom and Dad looked blank as dinner plates.

"Oh, for crying out loud!" Nan glared at Tim. "You can't expect them to believe that."

"I don't care if they believe it!" Tim looked like he was going to cry again.

There was only one thing to do. "Look, go fetch that knitting needle, okay? The one you dug up with the stump. We'll show them." As he scurried off obediently, she faced her parents with what she hoped was an authoritative air. "We discovered time travel. We knew it'd sound weird—and Gramma wouldn't believe us—so we've been experimenting so we can prove it."

"I see." There was a terrible flatness to Mom's voice. "And what time did you travel to?"

"Well—your wedding, for one. Remember the kids in shorts at the reception? I climbed the pecan tree and got in the window to fetch your suitcase, and Tim brought you some barbecue."

That got their attention. "Did Gramma tell you about that?" asked Dad, sharply.

"Nobody told us anything. We went." She told him what had happened as briefly as she could. "I can show you in my notebooks, but I bet you could remember if you tried."

"That little girl did have the Chadwell face," said Mom,

sounding odd, "but—I haven't thought about those kids in years. I don't remember their faces a bit."

"This isn't funny, Nan," said Dad, seriously.

"I know that. I didn't want to tell you yet, but what could I do, once Tim started blabbing?"

Tim returned, carrying the needle in its plastic bag. "I haven't made a poem on this."

"We'll have to make one up now." Nan reached for the bag, but he held it out of her reach. Oh, well. "I started one a while back. Let's see what I can remember."

"Poem?" said Mom, dubiously.

"For the spell," said Tim.

"It's not a spell!" snapped Nan. "I keep telling him this is science, not magic! But we do need a poem. I don't know why."

Mom and Dad exchanged glances, but they waited. Nan knew very well that most people wouldn't have. Not Gramma. Most likely not Big Daddy, either. Knowing they were waiting made the verse composing hard, but at last she and Tim cobbled something together, and he took the needle out of its bag.

"Okay," said Nan, "now, we all hold onto the needle and say the poem three times. And then we'll time travel. You might want to close your eyes. It's kind of dizzy."

"I think I'd rather see where I'm going," said Dad, wryly.

"Wait a minute!" said Tim. "If we do it here and it's

before the flood we'll appear inside the tree! Let's go down to the channel."

Nan had the sudden, sick sensation of a danger narrowly avoided. "Right. But not too far. We don't know when she lost the needle. The water might be high."

"Y'all are serious," said Mom, in a discovering voice.

"Of course we are! You think we'd play games now?" Nan demanded, affronted. They moved down the bank, and with some slips and hesitations, recited the poem together:

> Underneath the live oak
> Great-Gramma used to sit
> to watch her children playing
> and have a place to knit.
>
> She was a busy woman,
> needed reasons to sit still.
> You can't have too many stockings,
> and that truth would serve her well.
>
> The live oak tree is washed away,
> the children all are grown—
> and some of them are dead now—
> beneath a granite stone;
>
> and she wouldn't recognize us,
> if she saw us here today.
> We found her knitting needle,
> but Great-Gramma's far away.

The kaleidoscopic whirl and the ripple began on the third repetition of the last verse. Dad vanished. Mom yelped. Nan and Tim grabbed her with their free hands before she could drop her hold on the needle. Sun and moon and rain slipped past them, cleared, and left them in another bright, hot day. A clear-voiced dog was barking; and someone stopped singing "My Wild Irish Rose."

Mom looked around frantically. "Where's your dad?"

"I don't know," said Nan, around a lump of fear in her chest. "This never happened before."

"But we did it," Tim ventured, in a small voice. "See? This isn't when we were."

Their house was the only one in sight, except for an unfamiliar red roof up the creek and opposite. The trees were different and fewer, though more numerous than they would be when Nan visited on Halloween. The banks were too narrow, and a live oak with a woman sitting in a chair beneath it stood on a gentle point of land by the house. The dog—not the collie Nan half expected, but a hunting dog—stood with its toes over the bank, barking down at them. "Hush, Buglebell!" said the woman rising from the chair. "Don't be so rude." She laid a hand on the dog's neck. The other hand held a pair of knitting needles, from which dangled a nearly complete yellow bootie. The dog fell silent, watching them distrustfully. The woman smiled on them.

She was as pretty as Stella, with similar eyes, though her hair was lighter and her body shapeless and swollen

179

under her waistless, knee-length dress. Her hair was pulled back and curled on the sides beneath a broad, shabby straw hat with artificial flowers on the brim. A little girl, about three years old, stumbled against her legs, clinging to the skirt. A boy of about five, in knickers, galloped around the yard on a stick horse, scattering chickens as he went. Great-Gramma said, "Never mind Buglebell. She takes her responsibilities seriously."

Nan looked at Mom, round eyed and paler than ever, and realized she wasn't going to answer. Nan hurried to fill the gap. "Uh—ma'am—have you seen a man in a gray suit?"

"No," said Great-Gramma. "But then, I've been watching my kids. Buglebell hasn't barked any."

"I guess we better go back the other way, then." Nan looked at Mom. It would look funny if the kids did all the talking.

Mom licked her lips, and said, in a voice not at all like her own, "I hope—we're not trespassing, are we?"

"Not really." Nan wondered how they looked to those big, familiar eyes. Their clothes were too dark on this bright day, Mom's skirt was too long and Nan's too short, and Tim looked nothing at all like the pictures of boys in Gramma's old books. "My husband's company owns most of the land around here, but the idea is to sell the lots and develop them, so we don't discourage visitors. Did you lose your husband exploring?"

"Yes, ma'am."

"Well, there's a road right here"—pointing toward the street—"and one across the creek, and a footpath back that way. Perhaps he took one of those."

"The footpath, I imagine," said Mom, gathering up the children's hands. Tim still clutched the knitting needle. "Well—um—thank you."

They found the footpath soon, running along the bank toward a distant house Nan recognized—an ornate, bay-windowed place that Nan liked, even though it had been made into apartments. Tim looked over his shoulder. "She's sitting under the tree again."

Mom sat on the ground in the shade of a huisache and wiped her forehead with a shaking hand. "That was—that was my gramma. She was awful young, but I'd know her anywhere. But—"

"But she didn't know you." Nan sat close beside her in sympathy. "That's pretty awful."

"You and Gramma and Dad looked at us that way at your wedding," said Tim. "We didn't like it."

"And that was Aunt Becky, and Uncle Jake, and—" Mom shook her head helplessly. "And she was pregnant with my mother!"

"Hey, you think so?" Nan hadn't thought of that. "Neat!"

"Where's Dad?" Tim looked at Nan as if expecting her to pull an answer out of her sleeve.

"Well—I hope—Remember how I couldn't get this to work on Livvy and Marge? Maybe only the family—you

181

know, Big Daddy's family, that belong to this house—
maybe it's just us that can do it, and we left him behind."

"I think we'd better go see," said Mom, recovering some
of her authority. "How do you get back?"

"Well, mostly you just want to. But we better move
down in the creek again. We don't move in space, and I
think we're in the middle of somebody's backyard."

They moved down by the water—which was as insig-
nificant looking now as it would be in sixty-eight years—
and held hands as they went through the Wizard of Oz
no-place-like-home routine. Mom laughed nervously, but
ceased when the ripple hit her and the world fragmented.
When things settled down, they were knee high in burrs,
the neighborhood was full of houses, and someone was
playing a radio too loud on a Spanish-language station.

Dad ran toward them. Nan had never seen him fright-
ened before; it took her a moment to recognize the expression. "This is too weird," he said, after he had felt all of
them to make sure they were solid. "You—melted away.
Like a reflection when you drop a rock in the water. And
I was still gawking around like a dummy, trying to figure
what to do, when the air over here rippled, and—what
happened?"

"We—I don't know," said Mom. "We seemed to go
back in time for a neighborly chat with my grandmother
while she was pregnant with my mother. I don't want to
talk about it. Not right now."

"Charity, we can't not talk about it!"

"I know." She laid her hands on his chest. Nan could see them still shaking, white against dark gray. "But—not now. Okay? Tomorrow, or—sometime."

"You'll want my notebooks," said Nan.

Mom looked at her, as if surprised to hear from her, and smiled hesitantly. "Yes. Your notebooks. Why don't we go collect them now?"

They returned to the house in silence. Nan and Tim took them to the artifact display in the sewing room. Here Bob and Stella came upon them, looking over pottery fragments and rusted cans.

"I hate to bother you," said Stella, "but the lawyer wants to know when you're going back to the Mideast."

"Middle of next week," said Dad. "He want us to sign stuff?"

"Yes." Stella's eyes were red and watery, and her voice thin. "It seems so heartless to think about the will right now!"

"Mom wouldn't think so," said Mom, with a faint smile. "She'd tell you to buck up and be sensible."

"Is the house in Gramma's will?" asked Nan, struck by a sudden fear. If she'd left it to the wrong person—someone who'd sell it—

"Stella gets it," said Bob. "That's why she feels guilty. She keeps rearranging furniture in her head between bouts of crying."

"I wanted a house," said Stella, "a house like this one —but not if Gramma had to die for me to get it!"

"She didn't," said Mom. "When she offered to take Nan and Tim while we were on the dig, she said she'd been planning to rent y'all the house cheap, as a birthday present, but it wouldn't hurt you to wait another year."

"She did?" Stella blinked rapidly.

"Why not? It was too big just for her, anyway. That's what Big Daddy did for her, when he was making all that money after the war and your Grampa proved he was a bad businessman. She said Big Daddy built this house to shelter his family, and it should be here for whoever needed it most."

They were all quiet. It seemed to Nan that the room was full—of sunlight, of grief, of something wonderful that had always been there without her noticing. She remembered Big Daddy holding her as he pulled her out of the flood—Great-Gramma swollen and happy-eyed—Gramma, planning how to take care of everybody, even after she wasn't around anymore.

But of course, she was still around. She was in the past, that was all—just like all of them, only everyone in this room existed in the present as well—Nan began to feel dizzy.

"So maybe when I'm a poor poet you can rent me this house cheap?" asked Tim. "That way I wouldn't have to sleep in the park just because Nan got mad at me."

That startled a laugh out of all of them—to Tim's indignation. The world returned to normal. Great-Uncle

Ben walked by the door and Mom went to speak to him; Dad and Bob soothed Tim's ruffled feelings; and Nan found herself alone with Stella. "I'm glad you're getting the house," she said. "Do you get everything in it, too?"

"Oh—mostly."

"What about Grampa's pictures?"

Stella smiled sadly. "She talked to me about them, when Grampa died. She said she'd leave them all to our moms, but if other people wanted any they needed to be generous. Are there any particular ones you'd like to keep?"

"Just *The Spirit of the Place*. You think they'll let me?"

"I don't see why not."

Aunt Faith bustled in. "Uncle Ben wants us to get a picture made—says this much of the family may never be together again in his lifetime."

"Coming," said Stella. "Do you want the upstairs beds moved to your house tonight? Seems to me the sooner we get Nan and Tim settled in, the better everybody'll feel. In fact, I'm not sure we shouldn't keep them here—"

"With your weird schedules? No, once I get the junk out of the sun-room everything'll be fine. I'm looking forward to having them."

Nan followed them into the living room, where Mary Beth arranged the family according to height in front of the fireplace, while Great-Uncle Ben instructed someone from church in the complexities of one of Grampa's cameras. Nan let herself be directed into place in the front

185

row—beside Tim, in front of Mom and Dad, two removes from a sniffling, skinny Aunt Hope. She had looked better in love beads. Nan stared down the camera, making no attempt to adjust her face, and thinking of the grandchild who—in this very room, maybe—would look into this picture, and see herself (himself?) reflected by the past.